CARRI

A SHORT STEAMPUNK ADVENTURE

SHELLEY ADINA

Moonshell
Books

Publisher's Note: This is a work of science fiction and fantasy. Names, characters, places, and incidents are a product of the author's imagination. Locales and public names are sometimes used for atmospheric purposes. Any resemblance to actual people, living or dead, or to businesses, companies, events, institutions, or locales is completely coincidental.

Cover art by Seedlings Online. Images from Shutterstock, used under license.

Carrick House / Shelley Adina—1st ed.

ISBN 978-1-939087-80-5

❀ Created with Vellum

INTRODUCTION

Who said life is but a dream after the wedding?

Married eight months, Lady Claire Trevelyan and Dr. Andrew Malvern are blissfully working together on a new invention, and providing a home for a collection of street sparrows. Then Claire's mother, the redoubtable Lady Jermyn, arrives with her family in tow and expects to stay indefinitely ... Peony Churchill turns up on the doorstep with valise in hand ... and raffish cousin Claude comes for a visit ...

While separately any of these would be most welcome, together they are overwhelming. Claire and Andrew flee to *Athena* for a bit of breathing room. But the last thing they expect is to have their airship hijacked ... with Claire's little brother Nicholas still aboard ...

If you like old-fashioned adventure, brave women, clever children, and strong-willed chickens, you'll love this short story set in the Magnificent Devices world. *Fangs for the*

Fantasy says Claire is "a wonderful main character (one of my favourites in the genre)" and the series has "a great sense of Victorian style and language that's both fun and beautiful to read."

For Bella Andre

CARRICK HOUSE

CHAPTER 1

A PIGEON ARRIVES

August 1895
London

$\mathcal{L}$ ady, a pigeon's come from the Canadas. It's from Willie's mum."

In the drawing room at 23 Wilton Crescent, Lady Claire Trevelyan Malvern took the letter from her eight-year-old ward Lucy, recognizing the decisive hand of Davina, Countess Dunsmuir. The envelope was slightly damp, probably because of its journey from Southampton inside the pigeon's brass carrying cavity. "Thank you, darling."

One was supposed to use the tube system of the Royal Mail once the intercontinental transport airships—on which the pigeons piggybacked for long distances—moored on English soil. But her household had most illegally rigged a communications cage at the top of Carrick House for her private correspondence, it being of the sort that ought not to be perused by phlegmatic postal inspectors.

In six years, they had not been found out.

She settled into her favorite corner of the sofa and began to read, a glass of fine tawny port on the table at her elbow. Lucy and their other wards—all former street sparrows—lay on the rug or curled up on the sofa with her, the older ones reading, the younger ones playing with a tin airship whose propellers really spun.

Her husband, Andrew, relaxed in the wing chair, proofing a monograph that was to be published in a few months' time, his pencil stuck behind one ear.

Claire still marveled at the changes wrought in her life since she was seventeen. Everything had begun that night six years ago when the Arabian Bubble had burst. The subsequent financial crisis had proved once and for all that the combustion engine could not compete with steam. It had also proved that her father, Viscount St. Ives, had been the next thing to a confidence man and had helped to defraud thousands of investors. The ensuing riots had driven her from this very house in Belgravia. She had departed in fear, forced to live on the streets, and each time she'd come back, she'd been a different woman. A street sparrow. An adventurer. A student. Then a surrogate parent. A member of the Royal Society of Engineers. And as of eight months ago, Andrew's wife.

Through it all, in her heart she remained what the children had called her first—the Lady of Devices.

She'd faced many a challenge in those days. But this evening, by the time she reached the middle of Davina's letter, it was clear that a challenge of a different kind was about to call upon her resources. She glanced up from the page to Lewis Protheroe. The young man was standing upon the hearth, one shoulder against the mantel. With his fingers loose around the short stem of his empty glass, he waved it as he argued some point of business with Snouts.

No matter how serious that business might be, poor Lewis would be utterly unprepared for this news.

Oh, dear.

In the spring, all of society had witnessed his gentle, diffident pursuit of the lovely Emma Makepeace, who had arrived from the Fifteen Colonies and become the toast of London's ballrooms.

And now we are told Miss Makepeace is dead, that lovely girl who brought such delight to us all. I have it from Alice and Ian Hollys that a young lady of Maggie's acquaintance is helping to discover the villain who has killed her. Do you know the Miss Lindens? They are brave indeed to take on the solution of this tragedy.

I have written to the elder, Daisy, to tell her what I know of Miss Makepeace and her appalling father, but I thought you should know of her passing as well, since she was known to you and Lewis. Be as gentle as you can when you tell him. One never knows with matters of the heart, but I suspect his intentions were honorable and true. I have rather a soft spot for the young man. I will never forget his and Third Engineer Terwilliger's kindness to my Will in those dark days when I believed my boy to be dead.

Claire's acquaintance with Miss Makepeace had not been a deep one. On the rare occasions she and Andrew had attended a ball this past spring, they might smile and converse, exchanging brief pleasantries as people do when they cannot hear themselves over the racket. But now, as she watched Lewis, her throat tightened. Her heart might ache for him, but his would take the worst of the blow.

Smiling at something Snouts had said, he glanced at Claire as if to include her in the joke.

Their gazes locked.

"Lady, what is it?" The base of his glass clacked on the oak mantel. He crossed the carpet to her, kneeling to look up into her face. "Is there bad news? Has something happened to Lady Dunsmuir? To our Willie?"

Andrew had lowered his proofs, and she could feel his alarm from here. She must not falter or show any less courage than she would expect of Lewis if their situations were reversed. "The Dunsmuirs are all well," she said for her husband's sake. "But Lewis, Davina has news that concerns you."

"Me?" In his surprise, he stood. It seemed to Claire that once on his feet, he braced himself. "What can she possibly say of me?"

"You must be brave, dear." She handed him the letter, her heart squeezing with sympathy. There was nothing she could do but what she had always done—given the ones who trusted her the unvarnished truth, and then a shoulder to support and comfort them afterward.

She met Andrew's gaze and between them there flashed an entire conversation, the gist of which was, *I will handle this, dearest. Some things require a woman's touch.*

Lewis's gaze flashed down the page—stalled—began again. Then, as though thrusting away the awful truth, he flung out an arm, tossing the letter on the mantel. His wrist hit the empty glass. It crashed to the tile hearth, shattering glittering bits of crystal everywhere.

Lewis, always so careful to be a good example around the smaller children, choked out a curse and knelt to sweep up the shards with his bare hands.

"Lewis—no—" Claire's skirts got in the way in her hurry to reach him. But it was already too late. "Take my handkerchief. Your hand is bleeding."

"Clumsy—such a fool—"

Could a heart hold such pain and still beat? Her eyes filled with hot tears. She touched Lewis's shoulder. "Come along. We—we must put some iodine on that cut."

"It's nothing."

She must get him through this somehow, and it could not be in front of the entire household. The only thing that came to mind was trite and useless. She said it anyway. "But it may become something. According to Dr. Pasteur's theories of infection. Please."

Lewis was no longer a child, too frightened and awed to disobey her. He was a man of twenty-one, a brilliant financier, the secret proprietor of the Gaius Club for whose rare memberships the sons of the richest Bloods fought.

And yet all she saw was the boy who had stood up to bullies and miscreants for her sake, and had become the first of the South Bank gang won to her side.

She would stand up for him now.

He must have seen the love and determination in her eyes, for he allowed her to lead him out of the room.

In the spacious, comfortable office that she shared with him and Andrew, she lost no time in dabbing iodine on the cut. She could hear the faint tinkle of someone sweeping up the glass on the hearth. Maggie, probably, who never waited to be asked when help was called for.

5

After Claire had covered the wound with a sticking plaster, she did not let go of his hand. "I knew you cared for Miss Makepeace, but I did not know how deeply."

A flicker of pain crossed his thin, sensitive face as he extricated his hand from both of hers. He turned his head away. "There is no keeping a secret from you, is there?" His voice held the ache she still felt in her own throat. "We used to think you had listening devices attached to all the walls. Perhaps you still do, only they are better concealed."

"The only one I have is in my heart," she said softly. "It does not take a listening device to see a man's pain when the woman he cared for meets such a terrible end."

Lewis's face crumpled despite his obvious attempts to be strong and manly. Well, as the children would say, nuts to that.

She took him in her arms, though he was now a head taller than she. His forehead fell to her shoulder and his body shook as he wept.

At length, he mastered himself and she pulled a handkerchief from her sleeve, handing it to him in silence. He blew his nose. "You will think me a fool, grieving a woman I barely knew. With whom I knew I had no chance."

"You are the last person I would ever think a fool, and she was the kind of woman who would be honored by your feelings for her."

No, Lewis had not been the only suitor to have been enchanted by Miss Makepeace's masses of golden hair and delightful laugh. Nor had he been the only one she had not permitted to call. However, as far as Claire knew, he had been the only one to be bodily ejected from the premises by her irate father.

She felt a chill at the thought of what he had told her about the roses. The bouquet of Persian roses he had cadged from the conservatory at Hatley House. The roses whose innocent heads had been cut off and strewn about the lawn.

"A few dances ... a conversation in a moonlit conservatory ... a chance meeting in a bookshop ... how can I feel this way with so little encouragement?"

"As Snouts might say, it's not the quantity, it's the quality. And along with the loss of the woman, you face the loss of the life you might have built together."

He nodded, his lashes still wet. "Perhaps that is the worst of it. I tell you, Lady, if caring for someone hurts like this, I may just avoid it in future."

"One is tempted. But I can say from experience that when the partner of your heart comes along, trying not to care is the least effective thing you can do."

"I don't see that happening."

"The heart heals at its own pace. It may not seem so now, but in time the smallest, silliest things may bring you comfort. Orange chiffon cake, for instance, was very helpful in my case."

A smile flickered to life, almost convincing. "The chickens, perhaps, might be in mine."

"Always." A moment passed before she found the courage to say, "That reminds me, I hear there is a hen and one or two chicks living rough in Hyde Park."

His head came up. Clearly, he was desperate enough for distraction to allow this silliness to serve. "Not near Rotten Row, I hope? They will be trampled, with all those ridiculous Blood horses galloping up and down."

"No, nearer the Long Water. I was thinking of an excursion tomorrow in hopes of finding them. My informants this afternoon were most insistent."

"Young Sophy and Chad, I suppose."

This was less a guess than simple deduction. These street sparrows were not members of the household, for she and Andrew had long ago run out of bedrooms. But they came to the back door now and again to bring her gossip and messages and news of a world that the Lady had once ruled. A world in which Mrs. Malvern, RSE, no longer found it quite so easy to move.

"Will you join the party?"

Lewis nodded, his shoulders straightening. "I think Mr. Thistlethwaite can manage without me for an hour."

"Your majordomo could manage an entire army blind-folded and you know it."

"That is why I hired him," Lewis said with a grain of satis-faction. "There is nothing like a retired sergeant-at-arms to whip some of the more spirited Bloods into submission. Espe-cially if they're suspected of cheating at cards. If there is anything he hates, it is a cheater."

The prospect of rescuing birds and whipping Blood heirs into a semblance of manners had cheered Lewis—or at least, he was allowing her to think so. Claire could only hope that the small joys of life would help him through the valley of the shadow.

Together, they returned to the drawing room. Andrew drew her to his side, sensing in that way he had that she needed him. As she leaned upon his strong shoulder, she real-ized that she must never lose sight of those unobtrusive joys.

For of such humble bricks was the house of happiness made.

THE FOLLOWING MORNING, at an hour so early the fashionable would not yet have had their breakfasts, Claire, Lewis, and the young ones located the hen and her chicks by following the sound of shouts and cheers. Several boys were amusing themselves by tossing in her chicks, and then forcing the frantic hen into the water after them. With a roar, Lewis and Chad waded into the fray, laying into the miscreants with walking stick and fists and sending them bruised and running for their lives across the green.

Tenderly, Claire laid the shivering, terrified mother and her brood in a basket lined with cotton tea towels. Sophy scouted the shore, her mop of tight black curls practically standing on end with rage.

"I'm sure we saw four of the poor chicks, Lady," she called. "I'll 'ave a look about."

Sure enough, the fourth chick had taken refuge in a bank of sedge, and was rescued in a storm of peeps and flapping. But once in the basket, it settled quickly under its mother's breast, burrowing deep into her feathers despite its wet welcome.

"Well spotted, Sophy," Claire said on a breath of relief. "You have saved five lives today, you and Chad. I am proud of you."

"I'm glad we got here in time." Lewis put a hand on Chad's thin shoulder.

Startled, the boy looked up from the basket in surprise, his dark brown eyes widening even as his mahogany cheeks suffused with color at the unexpected gesture of affection.

"Me too, sir," he whispered. "No one deserves to be treated so, not even a dumb animal."

"You'll find chickens much more intelligent than that lot." Lewis jerked his chin in the direction the fleeing youths had gone. "Perhaps after we get them settled in the garden at Carrick House, and Granny Protheroe has found you both a bite to eat, you and I might have a word."

"Me, sir?" Chad's gaze became apprehensive. "Wot about?"

"It seems I may have an opening at the Gaius Club. I think you would do admirably."

The boy's jaw dropped, before he snapped it closed. "Can't, sir. Not all the way over in Mayfair. What would my sister do wivout me? Our patch is 'ere."

She elbowed him and hissed, "Are you mad? Take the job and never mind. I'll manage, same as always."

Claire picked up the basket and indicated they might begin the walk home, though every instinct urged her to leap in and offer suggestions and help. The club was Lewis's domain, and while he asked her and Andrew for advice now and again, he'd proven his own astonishing abilities so often that she suspected he did it merely so that they would feel welcome and included in his affairs.

"No females are allowed in any of the gentlemen's clubs, I'm afraid, not even as staff," Lewis said as they passed Hyde Park Corner. Even this early, someone was on the soapbox ranting about the evils of undersea dirigibles. "But let us talk it over after breakfast, shall we? No business decision was ever well made on an empty stomach."

"Claire!" called a voice behind them, and a young woman reined in a chestnut horse in a clatter of hooves. "Claire Malvern, it is you, is it not?"

With the handle of the basket in both hands, Claire turned in surprise. "Good heavens! Peony Churchill?"

The young lady slid from her side saddle and hitched up her brown velvet riding habit in one gloved hand. Her veiled top hat sat at a jaunty angle on the rich braided bundle of her hair, and her cheeks were flushed with exercise and pleasure. Claire barely had time to hand the basket to Sophy before she was gathered into Peony's lavender-scented embrace and kissed on both cheeks, French fashion.

"I hardly recognized you without a lightning rifle in the rear view," Peony said. "My goodness, how happy you look. Marriage suits you, does it?"

"It does," Claire said, still feeling slightly winded from surprise. "I never know if my letters are going to find you. I thought you were in Paris."

"That was ages ago, before I trekked out to the wilds of Cornwall for your wedding. I have been mainly in the Fifteen Colonies and the Canadas." Peony's lashes fluttered up. "Do introduce me to your friends."

Claire slipped an arm through hers. "Peony Churchill, may I introduce Lewis Protheroe, my private secretary, and our young friends Chad and Sophy Morton."

Peony held out her hand, and shook Lewis's, then Sophy's, then Chad's, effortlessly observing the rules of precedence as if she had not noticed the torn jacket, the dirty faces, or the ragged hems. Chad and Sophy accepted food at Carrick House, but their fierce pride would not allow them to take more. They made the rounds of the church charities for their clothing, and caught odd jobs where they could. Pickpocketing and games of chance would ensure the permanent closure of the back door, so as far as Claire knew, they had given them up.

Claire hoped that Lewis's kind offer would be the making of the boy, and she would need to find a solution for Sophy. They were compassionate, independent, and strong—exactly the sort who would do well if only they had a chance at making their living.

"Mr. Protheroe, I don't believe we met in the Canadas, did we?" Peony leaned over to look in the basket, then drew back as though it contained a snake. "That is a chicken. A live chicken."

"It is, miss. We have just rescued her," Sophy told her.

"My goodness, Claire, in some respects you have not changed at all. In others—" She tilted her head toward Claire's hand, with its trio of pearls set in gold on the fourth finger.

"You did not meet me on the voyage to the Canadas, no," Lewis said in reply, finally getting a word in edgewise. "Lady Claire asked me to come, but I preferred to look after her affairs here. As it turned out, that was the right decision."

"Look after her affairs," Peony repeated. She eyed him as though he had become very interesting indeed. "You must be much older than you look to have that kind of responsibility. That was nearly six years ago."

"Lewis is a most resourceful young man." Claire was unable to keep the quiet pride from her tone. "I think he must have been born with the ability to do arithmetic, and he never forgets a detail of business, especially when it comes to the stock market."

"Really." The horse walked along on its rein behind its mistress as though it might be quite used to this kind of interruption to its exercise. "Well then, Mr. Protheroe, if you ever tire of your present employment, perhaps I could convince you to advise me. I could certainly use it."

"That is a leading statement if ever I heard one," Claire said with a smile. "Peony, you must come to dinner. This evening, if you are not otherwise engaged. I want to catch up on every detail that you have so coyly left out of your letters."

"That would take much longer than one evening," Peony said in a sober tone that made Claire gaze at her in surprise. Then she brightened. "But I would love to come."

"Eight o'clock?"

"Perfect. Are you still at Carrick House?"

"Oh, yes. I own it now, if you remember. I'll send round a card, shall I?"

"Oh, goodness, let's not stand upon ceremony. I'll simply see you this evening." Swiftly, she reeled in the horse and Lewis offered his cupped hands as a mounting block. In a moment she was back in the saddle, smiling and supremely confident. "Good morning to you all."

Lewis and Chad watched in admiration as she nudged the chestnut to a canter. "Quite a looker, innit?" the latter said to no one in particular.

Lewis cleared his throat. "That is Miss Churchill to you. She is the Lady's friend."

"She c'n still be a looker. The Lady is."

"Don't be impertinent." Lewis took the basket from Sophy and they walked on in the direction of Wilton Crescent.

Claire smothered a smile. "Chad, have you ever heard of Miss Churchill's mother, Isobel?"

"Weren't she a spy?"

"She was not," Claire said with firmness. "She was working on behalf of the Nan'uk and other peoples in the Canadas, negotiating with Her Majesty's representatives to see that their rights and resources were not abused. As it happens, so was Lady Hollys's father, Mr. Chalmers."

"Lady Hollys has a father?" Sophy said in some surprise. "We ent never seen 'im."

"Everybody's got a father, you numpty." Chad elbowed her in the ribs.

She elbowed him back. "We don't. Not ever."

"In the beginning you must have," Lewis said. "Just like me. Granny Protheroe's son was my father, though I don't remember him or my mother. Granny brought me up."

"We brought up our own selfs," Sophy said proudly. "Once we run away from the work'ouse, that is."

The two of them ran on ahead, probably to break the news of their success in the rescue at the house. Claire and Lewis followed more slowly with the basket. The hen was looking less terrified and more resigned to her unexpected mode of travel, as long as it didn't involve water.

"Lewis, it just occurred to me that Miss Churchill was riding a horse," Claire said suddenly.

"I did notice a rather large beast in the vicinity," he replied with such gravity she was quite sure he used the same tone on inebriated Bloods at the club. "She is a fine rider."

"But Lewis, she is a Wit. Or was, the last I saw her. Only Bloods are stuffy enough to ride horses in the Row in this day and age. The rest of us drive landaus and high flyers and penny-farthings. That sort of thing."

"Perhaps she has changed, Lady."

"Perhaps." Claire fell silent. And how uncharacteristic was it that Peony had not wanted her card. Perhaps it wasn't the card at all. Perhaps she simply hadn't wanted to say where she was staying.

How very odd.

CHAPTER 2

LADY JERMYN, SIR RICHARD, NICHOLAS, AND PEONY ARRIVE

While Lewis took Sophie and Chad into the garden to introduce the hen and her chicks to the other members of the flock, Claire went down to the kitchen to tell Granny Protheroe there would be one more for dinner.

"Ah, milady, if you could see your way to finding me some help, that news would be a lot more welcome. I don't know what possessed us to let go of Charlie, I really don't."

"He was offered a position on *Swan*, Granny," Claire reminded her. "Sir Ian and Lady Hollys are very pleased with his work, and he has a chance to rise in the ranks of the fleet. You trained him well."

The elderly woman sighed. "That's the way of it, innit? You train 'em up proper and someone else snaps 'em up sure as can be. Our Alice'll lose him too, just you wait."

"Not, I hope, for some time." Claire regarded the chaos of the breakfast dishes, which little Lucy was attempting to address even though the frying pan was nearly as big as she was. "Granny, I may have a possibility for you. Lewis wishes to hire young Chad Morton at the club. What do you think of his sister as your assistant here?"

Granny scrubbed the big table with salt. "I think she'd make off with the silver soon as look at it."

"We have an agreement that thievery of all kinds will be suspended if a sparrow takes a meal here."

"And you trust them two?"

"I do."

Lucy looked over her shoulder, from her step-stool in front of the sink. "Sophy's all right, milady. She ent broke her promise, and she even asked could she join us at our lessons, maybe."

"Did she? That sounds promising." Claire had lost one or two to the streets once they realized the price of food and safety was knowledge. Everyone began with arithmetic, spelling, mechanics, and basic housekeeping no matter how old they were. After that came logic, chemistry, and history ... and employment. "There, Granny. With your permission, I shall ask her. She and Chad are in the garden with the new hen and her babies."

"It's your kitchen, milady," Granny said, the way she always did.

"No, Granny, it is yours," Claire replied, the way she knew she must.

"I'll have a word with her, then, but don't be surprised if she does a runner."

"Thank you, Granny." Claire took herself upstairs to the office, where Andrew applauded her idea. Then she told him how they had met with Peony.

"I shall be glad to see her," he said, tilting back in his

17

leather chair. "She doesn't stand on ceremony, does she? Admitting one has no engagements for the evening and accepting an invitation so promptly? No pride there."

"Merely the privilege of friendship."

A whoosh and a thump announced the arrival of a tube downstairs, and in a moment there was a knock on the open door.

Eighteen-year-old Maggie Polgarth, to whom Claire was as close as an elder sister, leaned in. "Lady? You have a letter from Lady Jermyn."

Would she ever hear her mother's name without this sinking of the stomach and this mental bracing for a gale? The former Lady St. Ives could comment upon the weather and still find a way to make Claire feel guilty about it. Now the wife of Sir Richard Jermyn, who had owned the estate bordering Gwynn Place all of Claire's life, her mother had found joy in her second marriage—and in the management of both properties. She held Gwynn Place in trust for seven-year-old Nicholas, Viscount St. Ives, Claire's little brother. Security had mellowed her a little, but not so much where her only daughter was concerned.

"Thank you, Maggie. Anything from Lizzie?"

"No," her ward said, frowning. "I can't think what is keeping her in Penzance—it is not as though Tigg is posted to St. Michael's Mount. He is still in the Canadas with the Dunsmuirs."

"Perhaps she is enjoying her week with your grandparents."

Maggie had been down to Cornwall the week before that with her cousin. Now her brows rose, delicate as the feelers of a butterfly. "Perhaps Hades has frozen over, and she is enjoying the skating."

"Maggie!" came from behind Andrew's engineering drawings, in the tones one employs when one is trying not to laugh.

"Well, we all know the truth," Maggie said a little defensively. "Our cousin Claude hinted he might descend on them. Perhaps he and she are guarding each other's backs. Which is hardly fair. She ought to bring him here for a visit, so that I can see him, too."

Maggie withdrew, leaving Claire with her mother's letter and a distinct feeling of *once more into the breach, dear friends.*

Dearest Claire,

By the time you receive this, we will be nearly upon your doorstep. We leave tomorrow for London, and trust there will be room for the three of us in our old home.

We are come up to town to do a little shopping, and to have dear Nicholas fitted for long pants. To think my baby is to have a tutor and begin his education! Mr. Alden Dean is a Cambridge man known to Sir Richard, so we have confidence in his ability to correctly mold our young viscount's mind.

I also have some news of a most personal and happy nature, but it is not to be committed to the post.

You may expect us in time for tea, as the Flying Dutchman *gets in to Paddington at ten past four. I suppose it is too much to expect that there might be a landau waiting for us, so we will resign ourselves to a hansom cab.*

Ever your loving
Mama

"Oh dear." Claire sank into her chair, the hand holding the letter falling into her lap in that boneless way that news of disaster brings.

Andrew lowered his drawings and straightened in alarm. "*More* bad news? What is it, dearest?"

"The very worst." She rolled her head to gaze at him. "My mother and Sir Richard are coming up to town and staying with us. They arrive this evening."

"Oh dear." Andrew sat back as though his spine had given out. "Do we have a place to put them?"

"Only our room, which of course was once my mother and father's. If Maggie bunks with Lucy, then you and I can sleep in her and Lizzie's room."

"Perhaps it is a good thing after all that Lizzie is in Cornwall. I am not sure what we should do if she were not."

"Nicholas is also coming, so at least there is a silver lining to this thundercloud. He can sleep in the boys' den upstairs. My mother will hate it, but he will love being one of the gang."

"They will look after him," Andrew agreed. "Did her ladyship say how long this visit would be?"

"Sadly, no. She hinted at no departure date, giving us nothing to look forward to."

Andrew pulled her to her feet and kissed her soundly. "I look forward to this." Another kiss. "And this." A third. "Daily."

Claire slipped her arms around his waist under his tweedy jacket. "I stand corrected."

A little later, smiling and slightly disheveled, she went to find Maggie and Granny Protheroe and warn them of the impending invasion. At least they had planned a huge steak pie for this evening, and there were plenty of buttered carrots, pickled beetroot, and rolls for—

Dinner.

"Oh, goodness." She came to a stop on the stairs. "I forgot all about Peony!" And she had no way to contact her, either, in order to warn her and give her time to cry off gracefully. The last time she and Peony had been in this house with her mother, they had come close to social disaster. Peony's mother, Isobel Churchill, was one of Lady Jermyn's least favorite people in the world, and her opinion was not likely to have softened with time and distance.

Never mind. The table sat twelve easily if all its leaves were in, and she could always ply her mother with wine if worse came to worst. They would manage.

Somehow.

Snouts, bless him, was never one to miss an opportunity to pilot the steam landau, so he took it down to the station to meet the train. Even Lady Jermyn could not complain about the tall young man who arranged for their luggage to be delivered and then showed them into the vehicle, even if his velvet embroidered waistcoat was slightly too gaudy for afternoon—and probably for evening, too.

"Mama." In the vestibule, Claire kissed her mother's cheek, was kissed by Sir Richard, and finally was able to snatch up Nicholas and whirl him about in sheer joy. "My darling, how glad I am to see you!"

"And I you, Clary," the little boy said, once his feet were back on the ground and he could hug her with both arms locked around her neck. "I have a pony! You must come down and see him. Polgarth sends his best love to you and to Maggie. And I saw our Lizzie yesterday and she says to say Claude is there and can he come up to town with her?"

"Yes!" Maggie said from the stairs, her eyes crinkled at the corners, so wide was her smile at both messages. "I shall send a tube tonight."

Andrew kissed his mother-in-law and shook hands with Sir Richard, who immediately followed him into the study muttering something about catching up on the latest scientific discoveries in the field of agriculture. Perhaps her stepfather would enjoy it. But it seemed to Claire he simply enjoyed the company of another man who shared his interests.

"How good you are to remember all my messages." Claire kissed her little brother soundly. "How is Polgarth? And his magnificent flock?"

"Claire, dear, really," her mother said on a sigh. "Must we be kept standing in the hall?"

She stood, her hand still in that of Nicholas. "I am sorry to be so remiss, Mama. Of course. You and Sir Richard are in your old room. You will wish to rest before dinner?"

"We are not as old as all that. But a little refreshment would be in order. You might send up tea. What time is dinner?"

"Eight. Oh, and we have guests." Claire plunged in. "You remember Peony Churchill?"

Her mother did not roll her eyes, because that would not be ladylike, but she certainly implored patience from Heaven. "Are you still in touch with that creature's daughter?"

"We have corresponded for years, Mama. She is in town from the Canadas, I understand."

"Wearing a bear skin and calico?"

"A very stylish brown velvet with cutwork trim, and a veiled riding hat, in fact. We saw her this morning, riding in Rotten Row."

"Riding? A horse?" Her mother's gaze sharpened. "Taken up Blood habits, has she? Or married above her station?"

"I am sure you will be able to ask her this evening." She squeezed her brother's hand. "Come along to the kitchen. Let us see what Granny Protheroe has to offer Mama."

"And us?"

"And us," she promised.

A tray was prepared and sent up, and then an hour later it was time to dress for dinner. As Andrew hooked her silk dinner bodice, Claire wished there were an armored corset one could snug around one's feelings on occasions like this.

"Is everyone to sit down to table, Lady?" Snouts asked in a low voice as she reached the landing and prepared to go down.

"Yes, certainly." His gaze seemed worried, a distinct contrast to the splendor of his waistcoat. "What are our numbers, Snouts?"

"Lucy, Dorrie, and both Alfreds. And Sophy and Chad are in the kitchen with Granny."

"Ah." She saw the difficulty now. "Perhaps the older of the Alfreds might keep them company while Granny Protheroe joins us. Peony would not care whether or not they had suitable clothes, but my mother certainly will."

"I'll tell them, Lady. They'll be just as happy."

"So would I, Snouts."

"Buck up, Lady. It can't last forever."

"Let us not tempt Fate."

The bell rang, and she hurried down to answer it herself. They did not employ a butler or footman, as everyone pitched in to help in her household, and whoever happened to be handy answered the door.

"Peony, dearest!" She hugged her friend, careful not to crush her dress. "Goodness, what a lovely frock. Paris?"

Peony shrugged off her velvet cloak and Claire hung it up. Her dress was peacock-blue silk with black ribbon trim around the low neckline. Shadow lace criscrossed the bodice, drawing attention to Peony's splendid figure, and she wore a choker made of four strands of pearls.

"Goodness, no. I had this one made in Edmonton."

Peony reached outside to bring something in from the step. A valise. She set it on the black and white chequered floor of the vestibule, pushing it nearly out of sight behind the umbrella stand. "Claire, forgive me—I wonder if—"

Andrew appeared in the drawing room doorway. "Peony, what a vision you are. My wife has been so looking forward to your visit, and so have I. It has been a long time." They shook hands while Claire dragged her gaze from the valise.

People did not bring luggage to dinner. Not unless they hoped to stay. But surely Mrs. Churchill still kept a house in town? Or at the very least a hotel suite?

The clink of glasses came from the drawing room. "I am not your only guest, I see," Peony said, a blush staining her cheeks. "Am I intruding?"

"Goodness, no, it's only family," Claire reassured her. "My mother and her husband, Sir Richard Jermyn, are down with my brother from Gwynn Place. They came today, with very little notice."

"Oh dear, and here am I, attempting the very same thing, even with your kind invitation. Please, might I have a word?"

"Of course." The prospect of not joining the party in the drawing room just yet was welcome, even if all this was a puzzle. "Come into the study."

It smelled faintly of Sir Richard's pipe, but not unpleasantly so. Peony did not sit, but rather rustled along the row of Andrew's books, touching spines with an uncharacteristic display of nerves. She stayed far from the windows, which overlooked the crescent.

"I suppose you are wondering about the valise in the hall."

Claire joined her in front of the shelves. "I am wondering, rather. Is everything all right, Peony?"

"I walked over here," she said, apropos of nothing.

"From ...?"

"From the hotel. I could not stay there another night, and did not wish to spend the money on a cab." She stopped fidgeting and clasped her hands, gazing into Claire's face in her old direct way. "Do you remember that night when you came to our house in Chelsea, asking if you might stay?"

"The night of the Arabian Bubble riots." She remembered it vividly. "You offered me a soft rug under the dining table, if memory serves. A delegation of Equimaux were staying, hoping for an audience with the Queen, and you hadn't a square foot of space to spare."

"Your memory is as good as mine. But I hope your response tonight will not be the same." She drew a breath. "I would happily accept a dining-room rug if I might impose upon you and Andrew long enough to spend the night."

"Has your home been overtaken by a rioting mob, too?" Claire was only half joking. "Have you nowhere else to go?"

"I haven't had a home here in years. But the answer to the second question is no, I don't."

CHAPTER 3

NEWS OF A NEW ARRIVAL

*H*ow could a young woman of means and resources have no refuge in a city she knew as well as London? But Claire heard her mother's voice across the hall asking where on earth she was, so there was no time to inquire.

"If you do not mind rather more Spartan accommodations than you are probably used to, of course we are delighted for you to stay."

Peony practically wilted with relief. "Oh, thank you, Claire."

"But I hope I am enough in your confidence that you will be able to tell me why it is necessary."

"As to that—"

But Andrew appeared in the doorway looking harried, and Claire had to draw on the role of hostess when she would much rather have remained in the comfortable role of friend.

At the dinner table, matters did not improve.

Lady St. Ives observed Granny Protheroe, the younger of the Alfreds, and Lucy bring in the dinner and then seat themselves with anticipation and pleasure. Claire made the introductions while Granny cut the pie and began passing dishes.

"I forget how understaffed the house is now." Lady Jermyn spooned a helping of pickled beetroot with a crinkled expression. "I have not met the people from belowstairs before, have I?"

"Are you running a school, Claire?" Sir Richard passed the bowl of chopped salad to Maggie on his right. "These are not the same children you brought down to visit, are they?"

"They are my wards, Sir Richard," she said, thankful that someone, at least, could ask a question without a prickly edge of criticism. "They come and go, but I am not training servants here. It is a school of sorts, I suppose, but the students are free to leave if they wish."

"I ent leaving," Alfred said, inhaling steak pie as if he might never see such a thing again. "Chemistry and mechanics? Them are a small price to pay for good grub and a real bed."

"Good heavens," Claire's mother said faintly. "Married eight months and still taking in street sparrows. Have you considered elocution lessons?"

"Claire has other priorities," Andrew said with affectionate pride. "She was in the midst of such a flock when I met her. It is one of the reasons she stole my heart." From his end of the table, he smiled, and Claire felt his warmth and reassurance all the way down its glossy length.

"Since we are on the subject of children," Sir Richard said jovially, "perhaps I might make an announcement."

Claire gazed from him to her mother. An announcement?

Mama had hinted at news in her letter last night. But somehow the subjects of children and Lady Jermyn jostled uncomfortably with one another.

"Might I propose a toast—to a future brother or sister for Claire and Nicholas!" His smile so wide his moustaches both bent upward, Sir Richard raised his glass of wine.

A brother or sister? Sir Richard had a daughter by his first wife, but she was busy turning out progeny in Norfolk, to the point where any toasts for her had become much more perfunctory than this. And Claire had not been in the habit of considering that lady her sister—she'd only met her once, at her mother's wedding to Sir Richard.

Like a matching pair of automatons, Claire and Andrew raised their glasses, then turned as one to gaze in silent question at Lady Jermyn.

Claire had never seen her mother blush before, and the sight confirmed the truth in a way words never could.

The astonishing truth.

"You—you are—in a delicate condition?" she finally managed. "You, Mama?"

"I am in the prime of life," her mother retorted, sounding a bit nettled. "There is no reason why I should not be."

No reason, other than that her eldest was turning twenty-four in October, and her youngest was just starting school.

"Felicitations, milady," said Granny Protheroe, which was a good thing, since such a civility had not entered Claire's head. "We wish you and Sir Richard good health and happiness."

"Yes," Andrew said, and raised his glass again. "To your very good health."

Lady Jermyn straightened and smiled under these happy attentions. "That is one of the reasons we have come up to town. To visit my physician in Harley Street."

"You are fit as a fiddle, my dear," her husband said. "Strong as a plough horse."

Her brow pleated in a pained expression, which she smoothed away by what appeared to be an effort of will. "Quite so, dear, but it does not hurt to be certain. And of course the quality of doctor here is far higher than those we find in Cornwall."

"Now, now—"

"I know you favor old Dr. Trevithick. But despite his being a family connection of ours, even you cannot say he is versed in modern methods."

"He does not still use leeches?" Andrew asked in some horror.

"No, of course not," Sir Richard said. "But he has saved many a life at the mines, and brought my own daughter into the world without a hitch."

Claire thought she had better join the conversation before it got out of hand. "When is the happy event to be, Mama?"

"After Christmas. I shall be attended by my own doctor here, of course."

"Here in London?"

"Here in Carrick House."

Into Claire's speechless silence, Andrew said, "Then you shall have the run of the place. For—dear me, how distressing —we will be in Munich at about that time, seeing Lizzie and Maggie over for the start of term."

Oh, bless him. Claire had been about to say, "We plan an

emergency voyage to the Antipodes," but Munich was a much better idea. And was even believable.

"Of course I do not expect you all to arrange your lives around me," her mother said with a stiffness that told Claire they had only succeeded in hurting her feelings. "We will do very well, and you will have a new member of the family to welcome you when you return."

"We shall so look forward to that." Maggie's smile held her delight. "Imagine, a new baby to snuggle and coo over."

"What about you, Claire?" boomed Sir Richard. "Almost a year and no announcements of this kind from you and Dr. Malvern?"

Claire's cheeks burned hot. Mama would never dream of asking such a personal question, but Sir Richard's being of country stock made it not only a natural question, but one she should have expected. Strangely, she was not offended by his interest. It was kindly meant, in the same way a bride took up matchmaking so that all her bridesmaids might find husbands as congenial as hers.

Though she was not sure she had ever suggested such a thing to Gloria or Alice.

"Not yet," she said as mildly as she could. "But when we do have something to announce along that line, we will waste no time in sharing it."

"Good, good," he said, leaning back and patting his stomach in a gesture she was quite sure meant that his belly was full, and nothing else. "Children bring such joy to a family."

"Even when they are not one's own," Peony said, catching little Lucy's eye and smiling.

Lucy smiled back, her lips stained pink with pickled beet-root, of which she was inordinately fond.

Lady Jermyn dabbed her lips with her napkin. "Shall we go through?"

"Through where?" Lucy asked, made bold enough to speak by Peony's attention.

Claire's mother quelled her with a look. "Claire? Miss Churchill?"

Andrew's expectant gaze made Claire remember her place—which was not meekly following her mother around as she made the house as much her own as it had been in years past. *This is our home. Mama is our guest, not its mistress. Accepting hospitality is one thing, but assuming the place of hostess is quite another.*

"Actually, Mama, we do not hold to old habits so much any more. Do be seated, and while the children clear, you can tell me of Gwynn Place and all the news from home."

"You do not leave the gentlemen to their port and cigars?" Lady Jermyn hesitated, then slowly resumed her seat when it became obvious that no one else was about to follow her. "How singular."

"Oh, it is still done at society tables," Peony put in, "but Claire, I believe, prefers dinner *en famille*. And I admire her for it."

"You are welcome to light a pipe in my study after dessert," Andrew said to Sir Richard, "but in all other areas of the house, we believe in unadulterated fresh air."

Snouts and Lewis engaged him in talk of horses and harvest, while Peony listened with evident pleasure to reports of people she did not know and household crises to which she had not been a party.

Even the most awkward evenings must eventually pass, and when the clock in the vestibule clanged ten, Claire applied herself to the task of finding room for all her unexpected guests.

"Miss Churchill is staying?" said Lady Jermyn in astonishment. "Why did no one tell me?"

"I suppose it did not occur to me," Claire said, counting beds in her head. "Please excuse me, Mama. I must do some rearranging upstairs."

"But why is she—"

Claire, however, was already halfway up to the third floor. Lewis bounded up the steps after her.

"Lady, Miss Churchill is welcome to my room. I can stay at the club."

"Oh, but Lewis—"

"It's no trouble. I have a suite there, you know. I just prefer to be at home with everyone, so I don't use it unless I have a reason to."

"Are you sure?"

"Of course. I'll just throw a few things into a bag. You'll send a tube if you need me?"

"I will. Oh, thank you, Lewis." She was in danger of falling on his neck with relief. "I had no idea what I was going to do. The rug under the dining table was beginning to look like a real possibility."

When she went to her room to see if her mother required anything, she found the bags had been delivered from the station and brought up—probably by the Alfreds.

Lady Jermyn drew her in and closed the door. "Now, Claire, I want to know what is going on. How can you live in such confusion? And how *can* you put up with that creature's daughter as a guest?"

With a deep breath, Claire forced down a spurt of impatience. "Peony is my friend, Mama, and has been since we were at St. Cecilia's together. Please do not speak of her in this way."

"But her mother is a spy and a known insurrectionist!"

"She is nothing of the sort, and besides, other than brief appearances before Parliament, she has not lived in England in some four years at least. You will not be tainted by the association, I assure you."

"My concern is not for myself, dear, naturally. My concern is for you. Do you not read the papers?"

This was not misplaced pride. This was honest apprehension, and the tight edges of Claire's impatience loosened slightly.

"Not lately, Mama. Andrew and I have been working long hours on a new invention. Have I told you about it?"

"Now is not the time for your gears and cogs. If you had been paying attention to the world outside the peculiar little backwater you have made of this house, you would know that Isobel Churchill has gone too far."

"Why, what has she done?" And fancy her mother knowing anything about it. For Gwynn Place could not be said to be anything *but* a backwater, lovely and beloved though it was.

"I suggest that you pay a call upon your friends the Dunsmuirs and ask them. *I* do not gossip, though the papers may."

"If you know something about my friend, Mama, I pray you will tell me now."

But her mother, always guaranteed to be maddening when

she was not terrifying, clamped shut her lips upon the truth and would say nothing further. Claire was obliged to kiss her good night and withdraw.

And then she went in search of Peony to have whatever it was from the horse's mouth.

CHAPTER 4

UNWELCOME NEWS ARRIVES

Claire knocked upon the door of Lewis's room, and when Peony bade her come in, closed it behind her. "Are you comfortable? Is there anything more you need?"

Peony had not yet undressed. "Only to be unhooked. Be a love?" Peony turned her back and Claire began to unfasten the hooks of her silk bodice. "Who have I displaced?" she said over her shoulder. "For this is certainly a man's room."

"Lewis Protheroe. And he does not mind in the least. He has resources elsewhere."

The lovely bodice fell open and Peony wriggled out of it with a sigh. Her corset, fortunately, was one of the front-opening ones, so Claire's assistance was no longer needed.

"That handsome boy. Such good conversation at dinner, and such a gentleman in the park this morning." Peony twinkled at her as she folded the bodice carefully and then stepped out of the skirts. "I feel positively daring, sleeping in a man's room without him."

Claire ignored this bit of worldly nonsense. "Lewis was

not born a gentleman, but he is one, in every way that matters."

Peony dropped her pose for the mask that it was. "I cannot imagine you associating with any other kind of man. When I heard you had engaged yourself to James Selwyn all those years ago, I was shocked." She added hastily, "Rest his soul."

"I shocked myself, I am afraid," Claire admitted. "The title passed to Peter Livingston, who married my friend Emilie Fragonard. Do you remember her?"

Peony sat upon the bed and shook her head. She had already taken her hair down, and several glossy braids fell over her shoulders.

"She is Lady Selwyn now, and you will be hard pressed to find a more grateful person for that than I."

Her friend laughed. "You are so refreshingly frank. One always knows where one stands with you, Claire."

Here was her opportunity. "Then perhaps you will tell me where you stand, dear. How does a lady of means find herself borrowing my private secretary's room?"

"Because your redoubtable mama has the master's room?"

Claire cocked an eyebrow at her.

Peony sighed. "Oh, very well. I knew I could not fob you off with flippancy forever. Friendship demands the truth, no matter how dusty the connection."

Did she really mean that? Surely she would not be deliberately hurtful. "I do not feel our friendship is dusty." Surely Claire could not have been deluding herself and cheerfully writing letters all this time to someone who didn't care whether she received them or not.

"Oh, dearest, I did not mean that." Peony pulled Claire down next to her on the bed. "I meant only that my own motives and actions are not as clear-eyed and above-board as yours."

"By that definition, I have certainly been dusty a time or two." What a relief that Peony had not changed so much that her faith in her might be misplaced. "Come. You must tell me what is going on. Mama has just informed me that I must read the papers more."

"I sometimes think we would all be happier if we did not read them." Peony's gaze seemed to settle on something much farther away than the framed daguerreotype of Claire and Andrew on their wedding day that hung on the wall of Lewis's room. "I am afraid my mother has got herself into hot water again, this time in Africa."

"Africa?" This was not at all what Claire had been expecting.

"Yes. It all has to do with diamonds and the peoples on whose lands the diamonds have been found. Naturally, the inhabitants want to be left alone to manage their own cities and governments. Apparently frustrated by his lack of success in the Canadas, Sir Cecil Rhodes has moved on to the southern part of Africa. He and my mother have engaged in a battle royal over it, with Her Majesty and Parliament laying bets on the sidelines as though it were a cricket match."

"But what has that to do with you?"

"Me? Oh, nothing. I thought you were wondering about what was in the papers."

Claire shook her head as though to clear it of this misunderstanding. "If anyone is capable of looking after herself, it is your mother. I was under the mistaken impression that the two events—the newspaper reports and your needing a place to stay—were linked."

"Only indirectly. You see, Mama and I have had a falling out. She has taken *Skylark* to Africa, instead of pacing the floors of Parliament waiting for Sir Cecil to come home to be shrieked at."

"Oh, I am sorry."

"About Mama pulling up ropes?"

"No, about your falling out."

"Only you would say that."

"It is the voice of experience. Mama and I fall out regularly. In fact, I feel another one coming on even now, like the very worst kind of cold."

"Stuffy and impenetrable, making communication difficult?"

"Precisely." But she would never say aloud that Lady Jermyn's dislike of Mrs. Churchill extended to Peony. Claire had a feeling that, once the visit to the doctor was concluded and it was clear that Claire would not be hurrying Peony on her way, a scene was coming that would result in the precipitate departure of one party or the other. Claire hated to be at odds with people, especially her family.

Perhaps, in a Herculean exercise of self-control, she might simply refuse to be rowed with. Though Lady Jermyn was completely capable of carrying on a row all by herself.

"My mother might be too far away at present for me to hear said shrieking," Peony went on after a moment, "but her bankers are certainly close enough to make life uncomfortable. In short, she has cut me off until I *see sense*."

Claire could practically see the italics form in the quiet lamplight. "About what?"

A hefty sigh. "The usual. Men."

Ah. This was something, at least, that Claire felt modestly equipped to deal with. "It is never *men*. It is always one man."

"Isn't it? Only, he is in Egypt and I am not. When I cabled to tell Mama I wished to take ship there to ... to straighten matters out, I was refused. When I said I had sufficient money in my account to hire a ship, she had it stopped."

"She can do that?" Claire said in surprise. "My mother has no idea about my finances, and has not since I was seventeen. And heaven help me, she never will."

"Ah, but you were independent then, and are married now. I am not in the least independent. In the past, this has not been a difficulty. But then ..." Peony turned her face away. "In the past, I was not in love."

"In love ... with a gentleman in Egypt?"

"He fled there a few months ago, and though he has not said so, I am quite certain she had something to do with it. I would not put it past her to—to *engineer* something in order to separate us. He has answered none of my letters, and Claire, I am terrified that something has happened to him."

"Surely not," Claire breathed. Poor Peony! "May I ask his name?"

"He is an angel," Peony said dreamily, clasping her hands upon her knee. "So handsome and accomplished and rich. We are perfectly matched in every way."

"Am I acquainted with him?"

"I do not imagine so. He is from Philadelphia."

"Oh, a Colonial. But you met here?"

"Here, and New York, and a handful of other places where we could manage it. He and his brother were on their world tour last year, and I, as you know, tend to take flight at a moment's notice."

An arrow of apprehension shot through Claire's stomach. No.

Not Peony, who could have any eligible man in London—and quite a number in the Fifteen Colonies and the Canadas, too. But the facts she had vouchsafed paralleled a little too closely a man they at Carrick House already knew.

"It sounds so exciting and romantic," she said with every appearance of encouraging these confidences. "But who is this paragon?"

"That is the fascinating part—the part that convinces me we were meant to be together. You have become such friends with Gloria Meriwether-Astor, which I never would have predicted when we were at school. In Lady Julia's circles, you know, they are still talking of the Worth wedding dress she gave you. How astonishing that Gloria married the Fremont railroad heir. I always thought she had set her cap for nothing less than a duke. Anyway, there we were, all going to school together, none of us suspecting that Fate was about to step in."

The facts fit together with a click to form a conclusion that Claire could not avoid. "Peony, you are not speaking of Gloria's cousin, Sydney Meriwether-Astor?"

Her friend's beautiful hazel eyes went wide. "Never say you are acquainted!"

"We are. In fact, he has been a guest in this very house." And been escorted out of it with a warning never to return.

"Claire!" Peony's face suffused with joy. "Then you know why I have fallen in love with him. And why my circumstances are miserable. For how can one love and be separated?"

Better to ask how one could love and be so completely

fortunate in one's mother, who saw more clearly than her daughter.

As Alice Chalmers would say, Sydney Meriwether-Astor was a skunk and Peony was well rid of him. But Alice was not here to say it. Nor could she relieve Claire of the burden of having to do so.

CLAIRE DID what she tended to do in moments of stress: bury herself in her work. She and Andrew were to give a lecture to the Royal Society of Engineers in a fortnight on their new invention—an engine that did not merely take supplemental energy from their Helios Membrane, but in fact was entirely powered by it. No one had yet been able to run a train or an airship on anything but steam. But coal and water were not only heavy, but also expensive. If their theories worked, an airship might be able to carry twice as much cargo if its engine were half the normal weight and powered by the sun.

Deep in Claire's mind was the memory of an earlier challenge to the dominance of steam. Of that dreadful night her father had shot himself in despair over the failure of the combustion engine. At least that engine had some similarities to the steam-powered design. The Apollo engine, as they were calling it, had even fewer.

Needless to say, they were putting their reputations on the line. But what was a reputation for if not to carry one where one had never been? This was Andrew's philosophy. And he was no stranger to risk.

Claire was more cautious, requesting test after test, tinkering for long hours into the night in their laboratory in

Orpington Close. The old warehouse had seen its share of changes since she had first begun work there as Andrew's secretary. No longer dark and smelling of fish, the posts and beams that dated from King Charles's time had been replaced with ironwork and glass. It was no accident that it reminded visitors of the Crystal Palace.

The glassworks that had once been situated next to Toll Cottage was now run by Snouts as managing director, and since all the glass had come from there, he regarded the laboratory as his personal showpiece. Now and again he brought a customer through on a tour, to be shown the Malverns' various inventions and offered tea and fruitcake.

Claire and Peony were just drawing on their gloves the next day when Sir Richard and Lady Jermyn arrived home from their visit to Harley Street.

"Claire, where are you off to?" her mother asked as she removed her coat. "It is nearly time for tea."

"Granny Protheroe will look after you, Mama. I am giving Peony a lift to a friend's, and then I will spend the evening at the laboratory."

"The laboratory? My dear, have you forgotten you have guests?" Lady Jermyn pointedly ignored Peony's presence in the hall.

"I do not have guests, Mama. I have family, and they are welcome to make themselves at home." She kissed her mother and touched the hatpin that secured her hat. It was the extra thick one that doubled as a weapon should she need it. In her reticule reposed a vial of gaseous capsaicin, and in her case of drawings was a small lightning pistol. While the Lady of Devices had retired, there were those in the streets of London who had not, and it never hurt to be prepared.

"Do you not want to know what the doctor said?" Sir Richard asked, his bushy eyebrows jumping like excited puppies.

"Oh ... yes, of course." She turned to her mother with what she hoped was an air of curiosity. "All is well, I trust?"

"I am certainly not going to discuss such things while standing in the hall. Come along and we'll talk about it over tea."

"Mama, we are on our way out."

"I see that. I also see that there are things more important to you than your family."

"Certainly not. But Andrew and I have a presentation to make to the Royal Society of Engineers, and time is running short."

Claire had not intended to annoy her, but it happened anyway. "Oh, very well. My news will keep until it is convenient for you to hear it."

Her mother seemed in perfect health, and Sir Richard was positively glowing with satisfaction, so it was clear that all was indeed well. And while she did look forward to a new brother or sister, its arrival was a long way off, and the Royal Society loomed in the immediate future.

"Very well, Mama. I shall look forward to hearing what the doctor had to say. Peony, shall we?" She had no sooner laid her hand upon the door handle than her mother huffed in exasperation.

"Oh, for heaven's sake. Always in such a hurry. You will be glad to hear that I am perfectly well, and expect the addition to our family at the end of January."

"January twenty-eighth," Sir Richard said, practically standing on his toes with delight.

"Oh, Mama, I am so pleased." Claire crossed the space between them in three quick steps and hugged her, though it took a moment before she unbent enough to hug her back. Then Claire kissed Sir Richard on the cheek. "Congratulations! We will return later, but I will try to be early. Perhaps nine o'clock."

"Nine? Goodness. We do not keep town hours in Cornwall. We shall be famished by then," Lady Jermyn said.

"Oh, you do not need to wait. Dinner is at six this evening, since Peony is going out as well. Granny will keep something for Andrew and me. She is used to it."

"Claire, I really must discuss this cook situation with you—"

"Good-bye, Mama!" Grasping Peony by the arm, she hustled her outside and then through the garden to the back of the house, where the landau was housed in its own mews.

Once she had ignited the boiler and reversed it out the doors, they were safely on their way. Peony tied on her hat with her chiffon driving scarf. "I thought we would never escape. Is your mother always so domineering?"

"Yes," Claire said, making the turn into Sloane Street at a higher speed than absolutely necessary. "Though of late I have been able to adapt."

"To my great admiration. Well done."

It did not take long to reach the house of Peony's friends in Knightsbridge, whom Claire did not know. "The Havershams are friends of Sydney's, too," Peony confided as she climbed out. "Oh, what a balm it is to be able to speak of him!"

Claire said nothing, only waved and pushed out the acceleration bar, bowling off down the road before she betrayed herself. Maybe she could dragoon someone into telling Peony for her. Snouts would do it cheerfully, she was sure.

"What a coward you are, Claire Malvern," she muttered to herself as she piloted the landau south across the bridge. "You can be of most service to your friend by saving her from years of unhappiness. Even if the cost is her friendship, it is not too high a price to pay."

Andrew did not have a better solution, though it was clear he had been thinking about it since the night before. They worked side by side in the laboratory, talking it over as they tightened screws and fitted plates.

"I am afraid I cannot escape it, dearest," Claire said at last. "I would be a poor friend indeed if I put my need for friendship before her happiness. I simply cannot allow her to continue this pursuit of Sydney Meriwether-Astor without all the facts. Not after what he did to Gloria. And certainly not when in Peony's absence, he was seen flirting openly with Emma Makepeace."

"Lewis might make that known to her," Andrew suggested.

"I cannot bring myself to suggest it," she said sadly, hauling on the wrench. "The reminder might be painful for him. It is too soon."

"At least if she is in possession of the truth, she can make up her own mind," he agreed. "Then what she chooses to do is out of our hands."

Once their work was done for the evening, they returned to Carrick House in time for a congratulatory glass of sherry before bed. Lewis had brought in a case of it from Spain for the club. Its quality was such that Lady Jermyn was slightly mollified about the delay in the celebrations.

Claire and Andrew retired early, more for a little privacy

than because either of them was weary from their labors. When one loved one's labor, it was not so much work as it was the fulfillment of a dream. Since Maggie and Lizzie's room had only single beds, there was not much more they could do but talk, anyway.

A falling-out with Lady Jermyn might be worth it if it meant returning to their own room sooner.

CHAPTER 5

NO SOLUTION PRESENTS ITSELF

$\mathcal{P}$eony must have come in very late, Claire thought, for she was not yet down when the family met in the dining room for breakfast. Lady Jermyn snapped her napkin out of the neat folds that Lucy took such pleasure in making, and laid it across her lap like a sword.

Oh, dear. What had upset her mother now?

"It is a sign of a very poor upbringing," Lady Jermyn said, apropos of nothing.

"What is, milady?" Snouts inquired, since Claire did not have the fortitude to ask.

"I am a very light sleeper, especially here in town, when I have become accustomed to the quiet of the country."

"I love the sounds of Gwynn Place," Maggie said, smiling with the memory of the place and people she loved. Her grandfather was the poultryman at the St. Ives estate—the most famous poultryman in all of Cornwall, in fact—and she wrote every week to her aunt Tressa and cousin Michael. "The boom of the combers on the strand, the celebrations of

Grandfather's hens after they lay their eggs, the bumbly buzz of bees in the rosemary and thyme in the kitchen garden. I love them all."

Lady Jermyn did not seem to appreciate this digression. "Yes, well, there are no such soothing sounds in London."

"But our chickens—"

"And to lie abed until noon! Disgraceful."

"The chickens do not lie abed until noon. Besides, it is not yet nine o'clock," Lucy pointed out. She was of a literal turn of mind, much as Lizzie had been, and still was.

Before her mother could turn her ire on the poor child, Claire decided she had better step in. "Mama, Peony is a grown woman and may keep whatever hours she pleases. It is no trouble to us."

"Presumably breakfast must be held for her?"

"Yes, but that is no different than holding dinner for Andrew or me. As I said yesterday, Granny Protheroe is quite used to it."

"That is another thing, Claire. I really must know why you insist that the belowstairs servants eat with the family. It is simply not done."

Claire took a firm grip on her temper. Here was the falling-out, and she must do her utmost to make sure it did not rebound upon the children. "I explained to you before, Mama, that my wards *are* family. They are being educated in the household arts as well as the academic ones, but that does not make them staff, or isolate them from Andrew and me."

"You are not educating Mrs. Protheroe, and yet she sits down to dinner with you. It will give her airs above her station."

Nicholas turned to Maggie, confused. "Is Granny Protheroe taking the train?"

"Not to my knowledge," she replied. "Which jam would you like—the raspberry or the marmalade?"

And in happy contemplation of this choice, the little boy ceased to listen to a conversation that made no sense to him.

Claire wished she could do the same.

"If Granny Protheroe ever met an air or a grace," Andrew said, "she wouldn't recognize it. But she is very happy to be close to Lewis. And not all good cooks are so unafraid to share their knowledge."

"I do miss Charlie," Snouts said into his mug of tea.

This was a frequent moan at the table lately, especially on days when Granny's arthritis bothered her and there was neither gravy nor Yorkshire pudding, for both required energetic stirring.

Lady Jermyn, receiving no satisfaction with household matters, returned to the subject of her irritation. "I wish you would not advertise your friendship with that young lady so markedly." The blade of her knife slapped butter back and forth on her toast. "What if society should hear that you have taken the daughter of an insurrectionist to your bosom?"

"Peony is welcome in the Dunsmuirs' bosom at Hatley House, Mama," Claire reminded her. "And Lady Dunsmuir, as you know, is a close confidante of the Queen. It is not likely that society will slight her, and if they did, I daresay it would not bother her in the least."

"Then she is as foolish as you are."

"Now, now, dear." Sir Richard patted his wife's shoulder. "Do not excite yourself. It isn't good for the baby."

"I am quite aware of what is good for the baby, Richard. I

have had two already." Her tone had taken on a tightness that caused Claire to brace herself.

"But that was some time ago, dear."

"Are you casting my *age* up to me?"

He was taking a breath to say something—which would be a mistake no matter what it was—when Claire saw that her mother's eyes were sheened over with tears.

And suddenly she wondered if there was more to her mother's temper than Peony's social habits, or Claire's domestic arrangements.

She put down her fork. "Mama, I wonder if you would take a turn with me in the square after breakfast? I find myself in need of your advice."

Her mother took as deep a breath as her corset would allow. "About household matters? For if so, it would be the first time you ever listened to me."

"No," she replied. "About something more personal. About … a matter of the heart."

Real interest sparked in Lady Jermyn's eyes at this unexpected prospect, and the red flags of temper in her cheeks faded to merely pink. "Why, certainly, Claire. I am happy to be of use, if you need me."

Thank goodness Andrew turned the conversation to grouse hunting, a subject of which Sir Richard was inordinately fond, and which required neither attention nor response from the female half of the table.

An hour later, Claire walked at her mother's side to Belgrave Square, with its pleasant lawn and laurel hedges. The sun was not quite at the meridian, but it was already warm enough to make Claire glad she had worn her linen walking suit rather than the gabardine, even if it was a perfect horror for wrinkles.

She was not sure how to broach the subject—in fact, she hadn't thought it through very carefully and was now regretting she'd said anything. At the same time, the prospect of her mother's being useful had changed the atmosphere at the table so markedly that she had to believe she had been right. Something was going on in her mother's mind. Whether she would allow Claire to pry was another question.

But Lady Jermyn took the broaching of subjects away from her as decidedly as she'd once removed the mother's helper when Claire had tried to take it apart. "So, Claire. What is this matter of the heart? You wished my advice?"

"I do, Mama. I am glad we are able to take a moment together."

Claire expected her to say, *With so many children around you, you've brought a lack of privacy upon yourself.* Instead, her mother said merely, "As am I, dear. Is everything all right between you and your husband? The first year of marriage can be as difficult as it is magical, when two different personalities must rub off their corners against one another."

This was a novel way of putting it, and one that made Claire smile. "Yes, perfectly all right. I have made the best choice for me, and have never been so happy."

"I am glad to hear it. I wonder what became of Sir Ian Hollys? He was interested in you at one time, was he not?"

"At one time," Claire allowed. "But he is much better suited to my friend Alice Chalmers. She is Lady Hollys now, and they fly together in Alice's ship, *Swan*. Sir Ian is semi-retired from the Royal Aeronautics Corps, you know, but Alice is a serving captain still."

"A woman," her mother remarked. "I read of it in the papers. What modern times we live in."

Since with Lady Jermyn this was a pejorative, Claire said nothing.

"If it is not your marriage, then, is it something more? You might not have been willing to speak of it openly to Sir Richard, but you may tell me. Are you expecting, too?"

The words gave Claire a jolt, right under her breastbone, as though her heart had leaped. "Goodness. No, indeed. At least, not that I know of. But if I were, of course I would be asking your advice."

"I should hope so." Her mother smiled, her gaze on the sky. "How people would talk if we were to be in such a condition at the same time."

She smiled, too, though her friends would do no such thing. "The matter I referred to does not concern me, but a friend who is in a most troublesome situation."

"Oh?"

"She is in love with a man whom I know for a fact to be a cad and a scoundrel. She is ready to abandon her family in order to be with him, and Mama, I do not know how to help her."

Lady Jermyn considered this for a moment. "Has she asked for help?"

"No, but I can see a day ahead when she may. And by then it may be too late."

"Is your friendship of the kind that can support honesty?"

"I would have thought so, but her infatuation for him is a serious barrier. I fear our friendship would be damaged, and all for nothing, for she would not believe me even if I did speak." Claire heard her frustration in her own voice.

"Then if you do not wish to leave her to the consequences of her own folly—as sometimes we must, Claire—then you need proof of his behavior that she will be forced to believe. Even if it costs you her friendship, at least she will not take a step that will make her unhappy."

"But I do not have proof." Not of a physical kind. "Only my own observations, and she may easily discount those as spite ... or even lies."

Her mother paced the gravel walk in silence, thinking. "What about another lady? Is there someone who might be prevailed upon to tell her story?"

"The only one I know of is dead, I am afraid. We just heard the news not long ago. It was a lady Lewis had been courting."

"Ah. The poor boy."

Claire believed she actually meant it.

"Can the man himself be induced to confess his crimes in your friend's hearing?"

"He is not in England, I am afraid. He is traveling, and P— my friend wishes to join him."

"Dear me. It is serious, then."

"On her side, at least. I am not at all convinced the gentleman has the ability to love anyone but himself, or that he possesses a heart at all. I know him, you see. He has even been a guest at Carrick House."

If she had expected a remark about the company she kept, Claire did not get it. Instead, they paced the gravel walk for another dozen steps, unhurried. Wrens circled the oak in the middle of the square, chirruping, and nannies pushed the prams of their charges toward the borders of the square, trickling away with the approach of luncheon.

"Then I am afraid you have only one choice, Claire," her

mother said at last. "Without solid proof, you have only your own observations and the reports of third parties, any of which, as you say, can be cast aside by a determined young woman in love. It seems to me that all you can do is keep your own counsel and be there for your friend when her heart is broken, as it must inevitably be."

"You do not think I should speak?" she asked in surprise. Her mother had never been one to keep her own silence when discretion was called for, after all.

"It is a fact that a woman in love is blind to her lover's faults, even when they are cast in her face by people she considers friends. It is almost as though she cannot listen. As though to do so would be a betrayal of herself and of her lover." Her mother paused, as though coming to a decision. "I have some experience in this, you see. Before I married your dear father."

It was so rarely that Lady Jermyn spoke aloud of Claire's father, the late Viscount St. Ives, that it was a moment before Claire could reply. "Did you lose a friendship over it?"

"I did, and I have regretted it. Particularly when I was proved wrong."

This was a revelation. And that she could confess being wrong to Claire was another.

"The parties in question were married twenty years ... before a riding accident claimed the man I was so adamant that my friend should not marry. There is some truth, you see, to the old adage that rakes make the best husbands and fathers, once love causes them to give up their wild ways."

Sydney Meriwether-Astor was certainly a rake, but Claire could not see love changing him enough to become a good husband or a father.

No man with a conscience would have attempted to upset Gloria's company and take it away from her, as he had. No man with integrity could have sent that train full of mechanicals to the Wild West, as he had. No man with compassion could have done it knowing thousands of people would die when the devices were used against them, as he had.

Oh, if only Alice or Gloria herself were here! Poor Emma Makepeace could speak for herself no longer, but both Alice and Gloria had been deeply involved and even wounded in the aftermath of Sydney's betrayal.

"Perhaps you are right, Mama," she said at last. "I cannot see my way through it. Perhaps the best course is to keep silent on the matter, and hope that she realizes the kind of man he is before it is too late."

Her mother tucked Claire's hand into the crook of her elbow and patted it. "Sometimes the most difficult thing a woman must do is to let someone she loves make her own decisions."

Leaning slightly toward one another, their shoulders touching, mother and daughter wended their way out of the square, and home.

CHAPTER 6

*T*wo evenings later, a tube arrived to tell them that Lizzie and Claude were taking their leave of their grandmother Seacombe, and boarding the *Flying Dutchman* the following day. They would arrive in time for tea.

"Oh, goodness." Claire looked up from the stiff stationery, still curled in the same shape as the tube. "We must rearrange ourselves again. Maggie, we will need to put Claude in Lewis's room. Perhaps you and Lizzie could bunk together, and Peony go in with Lucy? Or Lucy go in with Dorrie? I do not want poor Peony having to take refuge at an hotel."

"Of course, Lady, but don't forget there is Sophy now, too," Maggie said. "She came last night, and shared with Lucy. Chad has agreed to work for Lewis at the club, so Lewis took him when he left."

Claire put a hand to her hot cheek. She'd forgotten all about Sophy and Chad. Good heavens, this simply would not do.

"Darling, don't fret," Andrew said, rising to take her in his arms. "You and I will simply sleep on *Athena*. I confess I find it every bit as comfortable as our room here. And it is certainly quieter."

"Oh, Andrew, you are a genius." She hugged him with a surge of relief. This was why he was so highly regarded in Wit circles—his thinking had the gift of mobility, jumping over obstacles like a deer and landing with perfect balance. "That is exactly what we will do. In the landau we can be back and forth for breakfast in twenty minutes, and there will be accommodations for everyone here."

"Claire, may I speak to you?" As she looked up from the society pages of the *Evening Standard*, Lady Jermyn's face did not show the relief that Claire might have expected at such a happy plan. Despite their *rapprochement* of this morning, her essential character—and Claire's, too, of course—would not have changed.

"Of course, Mama. Let us go into the office."

Everyone was enjoying their after-dinner pastimes in the drawing room, so Claire was not about to send them all away. Not when Sophy—goodness, how had she overlooked the poor child?—still looked a little skittish and uncertain, as though someone might chase her out with a broom. Claire was not altogether sure she wouldn't scarper altogether, but Maggie was a steadying influence as the two perused the sections of the *Evening Standard* that Lady Jermyn had already discarded. An outsider might have thought they were reading aloud. In fact, Maggie was testing Sophy's ability with the letters to determine where her education should begin.

Peony was out at the theater with the Havershams, but

Claire would leave her a note telling her of their augmented numbers, and letting her know she would need to move up to the girls' floor.

Lady Jermyn followed her back to the office, where Claire sank onto the sofa under the window that overlooked the garden. She patted the embroidered cushions companionably. It would not do to sit behind her desk, and she certainly wouldn't permit her mother to do so. She braced herself for a lecture on her poor grip on her household.

Of course they could host more guests if there had not been a flock of street sparrows roosting here. But she and Andrew had their priorities. Guests could come and go in small numbers and feel no more effect from their hospitality than comfort and good cheer. But a boy or girl with willingness and aptitude could find their lives changed as a result of their stay. Claire was not about to give that up, no matter what her mother thought.

"What is it, Mama?" she asked as pleasantly as she could.

Her mother seated herself gracefully, the plum-colored pleats and draperies of her dinner dress spreading to either side. Her blond hair was caught up in a pair of jeweled combs, the pompadour style adding height to her straight-backed posture. Claire could only hope to possess such unconscious elegance when she herself reached the age of forty-four.

"I believe I owe you an apology, Claire."

This was so unexpected that Claire blinked, as though fireworks had gone off under her nose. "Whatever for?"

Her mother gazed at the far wall, where a map of the world was pinned and the major flight routes traced in green ink. "I confess that this pregnancy has had one effect that I did not anticipate. I find myself very short-tempered and liable to fly into a rage at a moment's notice. Poor Sir Richard. I feel quite sorry for him."

Since Claire had been dealing with her mother's temper for her entire life, she doubted that pregnancy had anything to do with it. "He loves you, Mama, and I'm sure forgives you immediately."

"Yes, he does. In any case, I wanted you to know that I am sorry if I have offended you or my son-in-law ... or in fact, anyone in your household."

Could this possibly include Peony? No, no. That would be stretching credulity. "I do not believe you have caused any offense, Mama. Please put it out of your mind."

Lady Jermyn nodded once. "In any case, it seems to be a very busy time for you, and I see our visit could have been timed a little better."

"Oh, no, I'm always glad to see you. You are my family, and our visits together are too few as it is."

"I agree. But with Elizabeth coming tomorrow, and her half-brother, I believe we shall board the train ourselves in the morning, and leave you a little more room."

Leave! But she had only had a few hours with Nicholas. And Andrew liked Sir Richard better and better each time they met. Their mutual view of the man as a phlegmatic, narrow-minded country squire had changed entirely as they had come to know one another as family.

"Oh no, Mama, please do not change your plans on our account," she begged. "Andrew and I will be perfectly comfortable aboard *Athena*. In fact, I had hoped that Nicholas might accompany us. What fun he will think it, to spend the night in his own bunk on an airship. Do you not agree?"

Lady Jermyn visibly wavered. "I do. And ... I must confess I had hoped to visit Madame du Barry to order some, er, more accommodating dresses. The ones I wore when I expected Nicholas are hopelessly outdated now."

Claire seized her opportunity. Fashion could bend even the most iron will. "Then of course you should stay for as long as you like. I do not know what Peony's plans are, but I am sure she will not be staying long. Certainly not as long as the week you have promised me."

How strange that the prospect that had caused her such despair only a few days ago was now all she wanted!

"And perhaps in the meanwhile I can think of a way to help you open her eyes about her choice of young man."

"Oh, if only you—*Mama!*"

Lady Jermyn rose gracefully. "Sometimes you are so transparent, Claire. I can detect a slip of the tongue as well as anyone." Smiling with delight at having put one over on her, she offered Claire her hand. "Come. Let us not leave our men to their own devices. We will find ourselves en route to the moors of Scotland for the shooting if we do not intervene soon."

Not with the presentation to the Royal Society looming over their heads next week, but Claire understood the sentiment perfectly. She allowed herself to be pulled out of her comfortable seat and they returned to the drawing room.

Claire had never had an apology from her mother in the whole of her life. Was it because Claire herself was a married woman now, and her mother saw her as an equal rather than an inconvenience?

She would certainly never have the nerve to ask. She could only hope this new understanding between them would last, and not be broken by the next flare of temper, whether brought on by pregnancy or simply two personalities that could not be more different.

At breakfast the next morning, there was again no sign of Peony.

Maggie seated herself with a snap of the skirts that showed her annoyance. "She is still asleep. But it is no wonder, since she woke me tiptoeing up the stairs at three o'clock. Do all Blood ladies keep such hours?"

First horses, now late hours—had her friend always been like this? "I never knew her to have the leanings of a Blood," Claire said. "She must have a very crowded social life. Perhaps when she comes down I can catch her. She has been here three or four days and we've hardly had a moment to talk."

In anyone else, Claire might have wondered if she were being taken advantage of—treated like an innkeeper instead of a friend. But not Peony. Surely not Peony. She had simply been out of town for some time and had more acquaintances than those in Wilton Crescent alone.

For a wonder, Lady Jermyn merely ate her sausage and kedgeree without comment, and then proposed she and Claire spend the day at the shops. Maggie, who needed to be outfitted for another year at the University of Munich, where she was studying genetics, was keen to go as well.

They were gone so long and so productively that when they returned at last, well after tea had been laid out, it was to discover Lizzie and Claude already there.

"Lady!" Lizzie flung herself into Claire's arms as if she had been gone a year and not merely two weeks. "How glad I am to see you!"

"And I you, darling." Laughing, Claire disentangled herself, kissed her soundly, and hugged Claude Seacombe. "Welcome, Claude. It has been ages since we've had a visit."

"Some might see that as an advantage." Claude grinned at her, and even Claire found that his raffish, silly charm was just the antidote for a worrying week. He was Lizzie's half-brother, and the two of them, one strong and determined, the other carefree and affectionate, made a very odd pair.

But there was no denying the love that had developed between him, Lizzie, and Maggie—nor denying Claude's willingness for Lizzie to immerse herself in a business degree so that she and not he might run the Seacombe Steamship Company once their widowed grandmother relaxed her grip on it.

"You mustn't let it be so long again," Claire admonished him with a smile. "You know we hope you consider Wilton Crescent your home."

She ignored Lady Jermyn's sniff and shake of the head, and told Lizzie where they would be sleeping.

Peony had gone to dinner with yet more friends. At least she had left a message with Lucy promising to see them at breakfast tomorrow.

"That's something, at least," Claire said to Andrew later, over her second cup of tea. "I am beginning to think she is a hallucination. A ghost, drifting in and out."

"She is real enough," Maggie admired her new hat in the mirror over the mantel, turning this way and that. "She makes such a racket coming in, no matter how late it is. Lizzie, what do you think?"

"I think it is most becoming." Lizzie sprawled on the sofa.

"How good it is to be home! I love Cornwall, but there is no getting around the fact that Grandmother is a trial."

"You may say that again." Claude stretched out his long legs toward the fire. "That was a capital tea. When is dinner?"

"At eight, dear," Lady Jermyn said. "You must pace yourself."

Nicholas and the younger of the Alfreds lay on the rug in front of the fire, playing with tin soldiers. "Clary, are we truly sleeping on the airship tonight?" he asked for the third time.

Claire set aside her tea and sank to the rug beside him. "To be sure. Won't it be an adventure?"

"Will we have to leave Mama?" His green eyes were a little anxious under a mop of auburn curls similar to her own. He had likely not been separated from their mother since her marriage some five years before.

"No indeed, my darling." She kissed the top of his head. "The farthest we will journey is to the end of the mooring rope —which is still some twenty feet. That is quite far enough."

"I have never slept on an airship." He beamed with satisfaction. "Can Alfred come?"

"Alfred has been aboard *Athena* before," she said, as though considering. "I think he would be a very suitable companion, if he wishes to come."

"That would be ripping, Lady!" the little boy cried, clearly having spent half an hour in Claude's company and picking up one or two of his more colorful expressions.

"You are of an age and there are two sleeping closets in your cabin, so it will be a delightful adventure."

"Sleeping closets?" Nicholas asked. "Not bunks, as we have upstairs?"

She shook her head gravely. "When one flies two or three thousand feet above land or sea, one is in the midst of clouds and winds. It can be like sailing on the ocean, where I understand a person can be tipped out of his bunk by a high wave."

The eyes of both Alfred and Nicholas grew huge.

"Therefore, the cabins are fitted with sleeping closets with sliding doors. We can tuck ourselves away and even if the ship should slew completely sideways, we will not fall out."

"You and Andrew sleep in a closet, too?" her brother asked.

"We do. Only it is wider, for there are two of us," she replied. "Also, when you go forward to the navigation gondola, you must wear a safety line. One never knows when we might hit a wind shear and lose five hundred feet in a matter of seconds."

"Good heavens, Claire," Lady Jermyn murmured. "You will frighten the child to death."

"I am not afraid," Nicholas said stoutly. "It is wise to be prepared for a voyage." He hesitated a moment. "But there will not be wind—wind—"

"Wind shear," supplied Alfred.

"Wind shear at twenty feet, will there?" His dear gaze searched hers for reassurance, and Claire saw Andrew bury a smile in his teacup.

"Certainly not," Claire said gently. "At most we will bob gently. The winds on the ground are generally not enough to disturb *Athena*. She is very well balanced and even keeled."

"And she is armed for battle," Alfred confided in what he likely thought was a whisper. "We shall be perfectly safe."

"The things you tell these children," Sir Richard said with a chuckle. "Before we know it, we shall be hearing of air pirates and sea battles."

Claire glanced at Andrew and now it was her turn to smother a smile. Dear Sir Richard. He had absolutely no idea about the stories they could tell.

And every word was true.

CHAPTER 7

LADY CLAIRE, ANDREW, NICHOLAS, AND ALFRED DEPART

*M*uch as Claire adored Carrick House, there was something about *Athena* that caused a change in her as soon as she boarded. Her back became straighter, her gaze more keen, as though they were about to pull up ropes and set off on another adventure such as the one that had brought the airship into her possession in the first place.

They were not going anywhere, of course. But she was the ship's captain, and both she and *Athena* knew it.

This evening was madly exciting for the little boys, who bounded up the gangway with their overnight valises and ran down the main corridor in search of their cabin. But for Claire and Andrew, boarding the ship was more of a relief. In the privacy of the captain's spacious cabin, with its drawers of charts, large viewing port, and cabinets of books, Andrew dropped the picnic basket in which Granny Protheroe had provided a midnight snack, and took Claire in his arms. "Alone at last."

"Thank merciful heavens."

They carried no valises, for they kept *Athena* stocked with everything needed for a voyage, including Claire's raiding rig, the lightning rifle, and several changes of clothes. The ground crew at the Carrick Airfield, which Claire owned, kept the ship's boiler full of water, her hopper with coal, and her galley with nonperishable supplies. While the likelihood of an emergency voyage was low these days, Claire took nothing for granted. If one of her friends were to need her at a moment's notice, and she could not come to their aid for want of a bit of food or a boiler full of water, she would never forgive herself.

Besides, now and again it was lovely to get away from the noise and smoke of London with Andrew and the children, and float over to the beaches of Norfolk or the Isle of Wight if the mood took them.

The midnight snack was laid out at ten o'clock, which was plenty late enough for two little boys. Though their eyes drooped over their cold roast beef, butter tarts, and sliced apples, they still protested having to go to bed. Nicholas did, anyway. Alfred had learned that one did not disobey the Lady and expect life to be comfortable afterward.

But eventually all fell quiet aboard *Athena*, and Claire and Andrew retired to their cabin. And there in each other's arms, they learned once again that no matter where they were, their true home was with each other.

THE HONORABLE CYRIL HAVERSHAM paid the hansom cab and hefted his own plus his two companions' valises, which made him stagger slightly under their weight.

Peony Churchill shook her head at him. He should not have had that final glass of wine, nor the shot of Caledonian whiskey that had followed it. His sister Charlotte, who had been one of Peony's best mates at St. Cecilia's, had wanted to bring her trunk and five hatboxes, but even after two glasses of wine, Peony had had the sense to put her foot down.

One, weight was a serious consideration on an airship. And two, when one was up to clandestine business, one could not be bumping about with trunks and hatboxes, to say nothing of finding someone to carry them at this hour who could also be trusted to keep his mouth shut.

"There it is," she said in a whisper, though at two in the morning there was no one at the airfield. There did not seem to be a night watchman, either, though he could be in a different part of it, or enjoying a cheroot by the river. "I wonder why they've got her out on such a long tether?"

The dark, elliptical shape of Claire's airship bobbed in the night sky, blotting out the stars with the generous curve of its deceptively shabby fuselage. Peony had seen *Athena*'s capabilities, though, and was not deceived. The ship was made to order for her purposes, being both unobtrusive and fast.

"Where?" Cyril said in a normal voice. "There are a dozen ships moored here."

"She just said the one on the long tether," Charlotte whispered impatiently, clearly still in a miff about the hatboxes. "And keep your voice down. We do not wish to be discovered."

"If we have permission to borrow the ship, what difference does it make whether we are discovered or not?" he demanded *sotto voce*. "And who is going to ask questions of a gentleman in any case?"

"Claire owns this airfield, so I imagine any of her ground crew might," Peony said briefly.

"Does she, now?" Cyril began to make his way through the maze of mooring lines toward *Athena*. "Singular."

Charlotte and Peony followed. "I do not *exactly* have permission to borrow it, in so many words," Peony finally admitted, now that they were here and the hack had gone. *No turning back.* "But she and I agree on nearly everything, and she is such a generous dear that she would deny me nothing. Especially in a matter of the heart."

Charlotte, in a tall hat made for riding and trimmed with an even taller brace of feathers, turned her head toward her, though all Peony could see in the light of the mooring lamps was an odd, elongated silhouette. "You mean she does not know we are taking it to Egypt?"

"Oh, she will," Peony assured them. "I sent a tube just before we left your town house. She will read it over breakfast."

"As long as she doesn't send the Royal Aeronautic Corps after us for stealing her ship," Cyril said.

"Of course not. She is the best friend I have in the world. Present company excepted, of course."

"Psst!" Moving her skirts out of the way first, Charlotte dropped to one knee in the deep shadow of a touring balloon. "There is the watchman!"

There followed an agonizing wait of at least five minutes as the night watchman strolled among the mooring lines not twenty feet away, testing one here and another there, checking under gangways and gazing down the chases between the short lines of ships. The touring balloon, however, being both small and inexpensive, did not seem to merit much attention, and he moved off without seeing them huddled behind the movable staircase under it.

What a stroke of luck, for Charlotte's blasted feathers stuck up in plain sight and would have been a dead giveaway.

"That was close," whispered Cyril.

"*Now* you decide to keep your voice down?" his sister hissed.

"He's gone," Peony told them. "Come. Quickly."

It took both brother and sister to haul *Athena* in, with Peony coiling rope neatly behind them.

"Gently," she cautioned. "We do not want the watchman to see her diving from the sky and come to investigate."

"Are you sure you can fly her?" Cyril asked.

"Of course." Did he think her a complete ninny, after three nights of careful (and increasingly inebriated) planning? "I learned in my mother's ship, *Skylark*. That is one of the reasons I am sure Claire will not mind my borrowing her. *Athena* will be in hands nearly as capable as her own."

When the gangway was less than a foot from the gravel—and when her fear of discovery was wound so tightly she could hardly draw breath—she released the bow rope and tied the belly rope to the ring in the ground in a quick-release knot. "Go astern. Make sure the lines are not secured," she ordered Cyril. "And keep quiet."

"Yes, Captain," he muttered, but he slid off into the dark.

She and Charlotte dropped their valises in the dining saloon instead of finding themselves a cabin right away. They had to get under way. With only four hours until the summer dawn, Peony wanted to be well over France before anyone at the airfield realized their employer's ship was missing and raised the alarm.

By then, of course, Claire would have read her letter, and while her forgiveness might take some time, Peony hoped that her understanding, at least, would be immediate.

For she could not stand to live another moment in this dreadful agony, not knowing what had happened to Sydney. She had no money to hire a ship, and Mama had taken *Skylark* an entire continent away.

Yes, she was the next thing to a thief. Yes, she was probably going to be sorry. Yes, she might even lose Claire's friendship. But if Claire was going to be stuffy and married and just like Mama, then perhaps their friendship was doomed.

Anyway, she was only borrowing *Athena*. A simple solution to a life-and-death problem. She must find Sydney—find him and help him—and then life would turn right side up once more. Then he would see the depth of her love and his own blindness. Then he would realize they were meant to be together, forever.

She would finally have a home and someone whose heart belonged to her entirely. Not to brave political theories that demanded so much compassion and time that there was nothing left for her.

She would be like Claire and take action, and on the other side she would find happiness.

In the engine room, the boilers were full and ready for travel. Was Claire going somewhere? She had said nothing about a voyage, probably because her martinet of a mother was causing her to go slightly batty. What was it about powerful mothers, anyway? But she had always liked Claire, and been happy when the other girl had been able to travel and find herself a little.

She was full of surprises, even if Peony hadn't seen much

of her in the last few years. Like marrying the most famous scientist of the age, for one. And being bosom friends with Davina Dunsmuir, who had the ear of the Queen, for another. Her letters were always entertaining, at any rate. Peony would have to remember to send a postcard from Egypt conveying her good news in a way that was both witty and brief.

When the pressure gauges signaled that all was ready, she returned to the navigation gondola. Charlotte had removed her hat, but that was the extent of her assistance.

"Go and tell Cyril to pull up ropes," she said.

A minute later, the ship bobbed as he stepped on the gangway, and she heard him close it. At least he had some experience. Perhaps Charlotte would be handier in the galley.

The Havershams joined her in the gondola. "Vanes vertical," she said clearly to the automaton intelligence system.

Nothing happened.

She repeated the command, with the same result.

"Is the ship asleep?" Charlotte wondered aloud. "Why isn't it listening? Ours always does what we tell it to."

And then with a sinking in her stomach, Peony remembered. "Oh, for heaven's sake. This ship was the prototype. For the intelligence system. It's so old that it only responds to Claire's voice."

"I can see why they tinkered with *that* technology," Cyril remarked. "Dashed inconvenient, what?"

"The question is, how does one fly it without being able to command it?" Charlotte asked.

Peony forced herself to relax her clenched teeth, heroically resisting the urge to swat Charlotte's hat off the navigation table for the simple satisfaction of seeing feathers fly. "One flies it manually, Charlotte."

She hunted for the vane lever and locked the forward ones into place. Presumably the lever beside it locked the rear set as well. She took the helm.

And for tradition's sake, she said, "Up ship!"

Athena fell up into the night sky, her bow already pointed toward the southern horizon.

CLAIRE CAME wide awake with the knowledge that three things were very wrong.

One, it was nearly dawn, for the air was cool—much cooler than it should be for August. Two, there was something odd about the behavior of the tether mooring *Athena* to the ground. And three, a small figure in a nightshirt stood at the side of the bed, looking in at her and Andrew.

The sound of the sleeping cabinet's door rolling back must have awakened her. She clutched the sheet to her chest as Andrew stirred. "Nicholas? What is it, darling? Are you ill?"

His lip trembled, and tears filled his eyes. "You s-said we wouldn't leave Mama, Clary." His breath hitched as he tried manfully not to sob.

"And we haven't." A quick glance out the viewing port showed a lightening sky, right where it should be.

Wait.

That was not the sky of London, with its trails of smoke and floating traffic, filled with the sounds of horns and hooves and huffing of steam vehicles. This was a vast, empty inverted bowl, deep blue on the top and lightening to yellow and pink at the bottom.

"Good heavens. Have we come unmoored?"

Heedless of her brother's sensibilities, she leaped from the bed and into her clothes. Fortunately, she hadn't come aboard last night in her dinner dress. A front-hooking corset and linen shirt, and the practical navy skirt she favored for laboratory work, took only a moment to put on.

The view out of the port made her gasp, and brought both Nicholas and Andrew over beside her. Andrew hopped in an attempt to get his other leg into his trousers, and tucked in his shirt.

"Great Caesar's ghost." Andrew gawked in a most unscientific manner. "How in heaven's name did we get to France?"

"I don't want to be in France. I want Mama!" The tears flowed over and little Nicholas began to cry, his nose pressed to the isinglass with its astonishing, unbelievable view.

The smooth patchwork of fields and forests and hedges scrolled away below them, so unlike those of England. The light strengthened moment by moment, now glinting silver on a river, now touching the gold on a church steeple, a village clustered tightly in its shadow.

Claire shook herself out of her horrified trance. "We are not adrift. I can hear the engines. The propellers are engaged on full. Andrew, I believe someone has stolen our ship."

Her lips firmed into a grim line as she crossed the cabin. Lifted the lightning rifle out of its rack in the closet. Pushed the lever in front of the trigger. Even though it had not been used in some time, there was nothing wrong with its oiled mechanisms or the energy cell that powered it.

The rifle began to hum.

CHAPTER 8

PEONY ATTEMPTS TO DEPART

For heaven's sake, everyone knows you must take the route over Spain," came an agitated female voice from the navigation gondola.

"Not true," a man's voice contradicted her. "You will save at least a day by going over the Alps, and time is of the essence. Or did I misunderstand?" This was said with the confidence of a man who did not believe himself to misunderstand very much at all.

"You did not misunderstand."

The third voice paralyzed Claire like a blue bolt from the lightning rifle, halting her stride, her heart, and a moment later, her belief that a friendship could survive nearly any danger.

"What you *have* misunderstood is your role here, and that is neither navigator nor captain." Peony Churchill's tone had risen to the shrillness of a police whistle.

Peony Churchill. On *Athena*. Stealing *Athena*.

Like a spectral lantern, Claire's memory illuminated moment after moment of their friendship—the Mount-Batting ball, the Firstwater mine, her own wedding. And then the flame guttered and dimmed, leaving the past in darkness.

Claire stepped through the portal, Andrew at her shoulder. "What you *all* misunderstand is that *I* am captain of this vessel, and you are trespassing. Peony Churchill, what is the meaning of this?"

For a full ten seconds, her friend stared at her while all the color leached from her face. Her two companions were similarly stricken speechless, as though Claire had been a spectral projection herself, and a terrifying one to boot.

In that, at least, they would be correct.

"Well?" she demanded.

Granted, this was Peony, whom she had believed she knew. But she did not know the other two, though the young lady looked vaguely familiar.

All the same, she did not thumb off the lightning rifle.

Peony's mouth worked ... and worked ... and at length words came out, sounding strangled. "Claire—what are you doing here?"

"I believe that is *our* question to ask," Andrew said. Then, when she said nothing more, he prompted, "Miss Churchill?"

"I—I thought—"

"Did you?" Claire asked. "Did you really? Never mind. Let us begin with the basics. What is your destination?"

"Egypt," said the young man, showing signs of recovering from his surprise. "I say, who are you?"

Claire did not dignify this idiocy with a reply. "Egypt," she said in a thoughtful tone. "Then may I deduce that you are mounting a rescue mission for Sydney Meriwether-Astor?"

"Goodness, Claire. Clever as always, I see."

Claire turned her head a degree or two to take in the young lady who had spoken. Beside her on the navigation table perched a hat with at least two feet of feathers—peacock, to match her velvet traveling dress. Velvet, to go to Egypt. She would expire of the heat before she stepped off the gangplank.

"Are we acquainted?" she asked coolly.

"Charlotte Haversham, don't you remember? From St. Cecilia's. We were in Chemistry of the Home together. This is my brother Cyril. He was at Heathbourne."

The only good memories Claire retained of her years at the London finishing school were Emilie Selwyn's friendship and the well-stocked chemistry laboratory. There, she'd learned how to make gaseous capsaicin bombs that had proven much more useful than the housewifery and deportment everyone else was learning.

She did not remember Charlotte Haversham, but she would certainly never forget her now. Or her brother. But since they were irrelevant to the present inquiry, she dismissed them both.

Peony was behind this. Claire had no doubt the other two were simply along for a lark and some moral support. Anyone who would wear velvet to Egypt could not possibly contribute anything useful to the endeavor.

Claire handed the rifle to her husband. "Please hold this, dearest, while I adjust our course."

With a smile, he took it and slipped it under his arm in a relaxed firing position. With one shoulder leaning on the iron frame of the portal, he looked as harmless as Cyril. But Claire had often had reason to be thankful that looks weren't everything.

On the navigation table, one corner held down by the hat, was a chart of the Mediterranean basin. Peony was still gripping the helm as though *Athena* required reminding of her course. Claire walked over to join her. "Excuse me, dear."

"Claire, wait—I can explain."

"Oh, I hope so. But for the moment, I must have the helm."

"No—please—he might be in terrible danger!"

"He might be," she agreed. "But you most certainly *will* be if you do not step aside and surrender the helm."

"How can you speak that way to me? I am your friend."

Claire gazed into her troubled hazel eyes. If she had hoped to find regret, or anything more noble than despairing resolve, she was disappointed. "No, I do not believe you are. For a friend would not have stolen my ship in the dead of night. A friend would not put me and mine in danger. And a friend would most assuredly move aside so that this appalling error in judgment might be rectified immediately."

Peony straightened, but still did not relinquish the helm. On the wheel, her knuckles turned white. "If you will just let me explain—"

"Release the helm and you may explain all you like."

"That's not what I mean."

"Peony," Claire said gently, "I will not ask you again."

"I say, are you threatening her?" Cyril, perceiving at last that this was indeed not a lark, came to life.

"Do not move." Andrew's voice was pleasant, but his gaze was not as he sighted down the barrel of the lightning rifle. "Technically, you are an air pirate, and I am well within my rights as first engineer of this vessel to shoot you where you stand."

Cyril's breath hitched and he froze. "Dashed inhospitable."

"And whose fault is that?"

To this there was no answer.

Claire's gaze had not moved from Peony. "Very well. There are one hundred miles yet to go before the Alps will force us to come about. I suggest you explain at roughly that speed."

Peony's face pulled downward into a mask of agony as she fought tears. "I could not wait, Claire. I have no money—Mama and *Skylark* are far away—I hoped you would understand if I merely borrowed *Athena* for a few days. We must find Sydney, and if he is in trouble, we must mount, as you say, a rescue. If he is not in trouble, then I must discover for good or ill whether his feelings for me are what they were in April. Claire, I swear I did not mean to cause you trouble."

"You do not consider air piracy to be trouble?" Claire asked with some disbelief.

"It is not air piracy! Please stop saying such unpleasant things. I simply borrowed the ship, the way I might borrow your comb or a beaded reticule. I did not imagine your generosity in small matters would fail so utterly in large ones."

"A reticule does not put the people I love in peril," Claire said.

"Do stop exaggerating. You are not in the least in danger."

"We would not dream of harming a hair on your head," said Charlotte.

"Unlike your husband, who is pointing that gun in a most threatening manner." Cyril had not taken his gaze from Andrew.

"Peony," Claire said with the last remaining shred of her

patience, "there are children on board. The parents of one do not know where he is. At this moment I can tell you for a fact that there is a woman in utter despair, believing that her only son has been kidnapped by villains, to be held for ransom."

"Why—why—that is preposterous," sputtered Cyril. "How were we to know there were children aboard?"

This was so ridiculous that the Havershams were once again ignored.

Claire gazed at the young woman whom she had so admired, and whose company she had so valued. Was this what Peony was reduced to? Putting a friendship to a painful end for the sake of a man?

If he had been a good man, Claire might have borne it. She might even have been convinced to assist. But to lose a friend for the sake of Sydney Meriwether-Astor, who was not good enough to clean Peony's boots?

Under her resolute, expectant gaze, Peony finally crumbled. "Oh, very well." She stepped away from the helm. "I hope you are happy in the knowledge that you have ruined my life, Claire."

"Steady on," Andrew said mildly. "You ought to be thanking my wife for saving you from a bounder and a rake."

Peony gasped. "How dare you!"

"He is quite right." Claire took the helm. "Nine, a one hundred eighty degree turn, please, heading north northeast."

The deck tilted slightly under their boots as *Athena* laid her shoulder to the wind and began the turn.

Claire checked the instruments, and when she was satisfied, went on, "We have personal experience with Sydney, you see. You mentioned his cousin to me the other day. Gloria.

She inherited the Meriwther-Astor Manufacturing Works in Philadelphia."

"Everyone knows that," Charlotte said in a tone that usually accompanies a roll of the eyes, though she did not seem to have the nerve to actually do so. "She is unimaginably rich now."

"If Sydney had succeeded in his plan to take the company away from her and install himself as its president, she might have become the vagabond he is today," Claire said. "But he did not succeed, thanks to Gloria's bravery and inner resources."

"I do not believe you." Peony's cheeks flushed with emotion, her eyes becoming brilliant with anger and unshed tears. "That is a scurrilous rumor and you should be ashamed of yourself for repeating it, never mind believing it."

"Would you like to see the letters from Gloria telling me of these events?" Claire raised her eyebrows at Peony. "Or perhaps the accounts in the newspapers would be more your style."

Athena came about and leveled out, her bow once again pointed toward England. "Nine, hold this course for two hundred miles. We will land at Carrick Airfield as usual."

Claire released the helm while Peony glared at her. This awful conversation was not yet over.

"I do not wish to add to your distress, but we have heard recently from Lady Dunsmuir that a young lady known to Sydney during his visit to London was expecting his child. I am only speculating, of course, but this may even be the reason he fled to Egypt."

"He was courting me!" Shaking with emotion, Peony

gripped the navigation table in an effort to hold herself upright. "Liar!"

"You and at least one other," Andrew put in. "And kindly apologize to my wife for that epithet."

"I shan't," Peony spat. Then, to Claire, "How can you hurt me in this way?"

"I do not want to, dear." Her voice broke. "A friend tells the truth, no matter how much it hurts."

"Cyril, what is the matter?" Charlotte said behind them, crossing the room to look into her brother's face. "You look positively ill."

He swallowed. "I say, old girl, it seems the game is up."

"What game?" Charlotte demanded. "What fresh nonsense is this? Can't you see poor Peony is in the depths of despair? To say nothing of our being held at gunpoint. Honestly, you are the most aggravating creature."

"Well, he swore me to secrecy. Not a lot a man can do but stand by his word, what?"

"And who might *he* be, old man?" Andrew asked.

Cyril did not seem to detect the edge of mockery in Andrew's tone. "Would you put that ruddy great gun down, please?" he said pettishly. "Dashed difficult to concentrate."

Andrew did not put it down, but rather draped it over his arm once more, in the manner of a country gentleman walking out to stalk the grouse.

This image must have reassured Cyril, for he turned to Peony, one hand extended as though to plead his case. "Mum was the word, you understand? Our set all knew, but he's such a delightful fellow it's easy to overlook his peccadilloes."

"You are speaking of Sydney?" Claire asked. "And his free ways with the female sex?"

"Exactly." Cyril looked pleased to be understood at last. "But of course our money was on Peony, here. She's a thoroughbred, and obviously the best choice for him. Money breeds money, what?"

"I haven't any money," Peony said in falling tones, like a child. "Mama controls the lot. But that is neither here nor there. Do you mean to tell me you knew I was not the only one to hold his heart? And you never said a word?"

"And precipitate a scene like this?" Cyril looked appalled. "Not bloody likely."

"Cyril!" Charlotte cried. "You *knew?*"

"Do keep up, old thing." He shook his head in her direction. "Didn't know about the little nipper coming along, but did know Sydney was mad gone on Emma Makepeace. Quite keen on Leonora Bakewell-Gosling, too. And, of course, he was one of Lady Julia's hangers-on." He colored in a most unbecoming way. "Isn't everyone?"

Peony was breathing more and more heavily with each revelation. "You *beast,*" she finally got out. "All of you. Beasts, every single one. I swear it is enough to make a woman join a convent."

"Steady on," he said. "No call for names."

Her color high, Peony seemed to be making a heroic effort to hold back, to not launch herself claws first at his eyes. After several deep breaths, she said in a strangled voice, "Claire, is there somewhere I might retire and not be disturbed? I find I need a little time to recover from the loss of *all my friends.*"

Claire's insides seemed to contract at the blow.

But a little time for Peony to think and recover her composure, if not the future she had once envisioned for herself, would be the best thing. With the helm secure, Claire had no fears for the ship, at least, for it would not respond to any voice but her own and Andrew's.

"Certainly, dear. Come this way. I believe there is a cabin free." When Cyril and Charlotte moved to accompany her, she held up a hand. "No. The two of you may go into the dining saloon."

"Is there a meal laid on?" Cyril's face reflected his hope at this good fortune.

"Certainly not," Andrew said. "But we can keep an eye on you there." He tilted his head in the direction of the saloon. "After you."

If Claire thought that an apology might be forthcoming from Peony for all the crimes she had committed in the name of love—or that she might show a sign of regret for the death of their friendship—she had to go without both. Peony preceded her into the empty cabin with an air of Anne Boleyn mounting the steps to the block, her head held high despite her pallor. Claire waited on the threshold a moment, then turned and closed the door softly behind her.

"Clary?" Still in their nightshirts, still barefoot, Nicholas and Alfred emerged cautiously from their cabin into the corridor. "Who are those people? Are we going home now?"

Alfred stood shoulder to shoulder with Nicholas, the pair of them stalwart as only little boys can be, though Claire knew they were both cold and frightened.

She knelt upon the polished wood of the deck and opened her arms to both boys. "They used to be friends of mine, darling, who have made a very great mistake," she murmured into brother's tousled hair. "They boarded the wrong airship in the dark and had no idea we were aboard. Wasn't that funny of them?"

"Mad, more like." Alfred said into her shoulder.

"Perhaps a little mad," she agreed. "Come. Get dressed, both of you, and we shall have our breakfast."

"And then can we go home?" Nicholas insisted.

She hugged him. "By the time we are finished eating, we will see the dome of Mr. Tesla's energy tower at Greenwich on the horizon. I promise."

CHAPTER 9

ATHENA ARRIVES

*T*he ground crew at Carrick Airfield had them tied down within minutes of their landing. They must have been on watch since the airship's unscheduled departure, and no doubt there was a pigeon full of puzzled questions still waiting in the ship's communications cage. Claire thought belatedly that she ought to have sent pigeons herself to the airfield and Carrick House, once she had the situation in hand and Peony was no longer careening headlong toward an uncertain goal and certain disgrace.

What they were was appallingly late for breakfast *en famille*. She sent a tube to let the household know that they were all right. Explanations could wait until Nicholas was safely reunited with Mama and Sir Richard.

She and Andrew were under the fuselage, performing their last landing checks of vanes and ropes, when Cyril Haversham sidled up. "Terribly sorry, old man, but any chance we might catch a lift into town?"

"I'm sorry, but with the valises and five passengers, the landau is at capacity." Andrew's tone held no regret whatsoever. "However, I can have one of the ground crew flag down a hansom cab."

Cyril looked disappointed. "Needs must, I suppose. But didn't I say? You won't have five, only four. Peony's not coming home with you. Deuced awkward. I expect she'll bunk at the pater's with us."

Claire had been wondering what on earth to do about Peony. There was certainly nothing in the etiquette books about how to treat a house guest who had attempted air piracy.

"Miss Churchill is at liberty to do as she pleases, of course." Andrew flagged one of the crew and requested that he hail a hansom. The boy jogged toward the airfield's wrought-iron passenger gate, which was typically haunted by one or two cabs.

While Andrew got the little boys settled in the landau with their overnight bags, Peony finally came down the gangway, valise in hand. So she had brought her belongings with her from Carrick House, all unseen. Perhaps she had anticipating a honeymoon under the Egyptian palms.

As she approached, Cyril and Charlotte faded away in the direction of the gate.

The breeze off the river fanned the tendrils of hair around Claire's face, bringing with it the scent of coated canvas and rope and engine oil. The scent she loved more than expensive perfume. The scent of her field, and *Athena*, and another safe return home.

Peony's half-boots crunched in the gravel as she stopped

just out of arms' reach. "Are you going to bring charges against us?" she asked bluntly.

Such a thing had not even occurred to her. Claire thought of the appalling consequences should she do so. The consequences were going to be bad enough for poor Peony as it was, choosing to drift away with people like Charlotte and Cyril for company.

"No, of course not."

"I suppose I must thank you for that."

Claire gazed at her. "You might simply have asked me to lend *Athena* to you, Peony. I know you are a capable captain, and she is an easy ship to manage even with such an ... inexperienced crew."

"I did ask you—for help, at least. But your dislike of Sydney was clear. I did not have the courage to ask for your ship."

How could it take more courage to steal a ship than simply to ask for it? "And now?"

"And now I find I must dig deep for courage of a different kind."

Was it poverty that worried her? She, to whom doors opened all over London? "If you are no longer pursuing Sydney, then it is likely Mrs. Churchill's heart will soften and she will release her grip upon your finances."

"That isn't what I meant." Peony looked out over the airfield.

Claire loved the ships and crews who moored here, each one coming from or going to somewhere different. A dozen kinds of adventure found temporary rest here, for repairs and refueling, for company and help.

But Peony did not seem to see what Claire saw. "Everyone

has a means to leave but me," she said, almost to herself. Then she shook her head. "No, I did not mean the courage to face poverty. I meant the kind that would allow me to offer you an apology. But I find I do not have that kind of—what did you used to call it? Spine."

Claire's throat ached—not from the wind, but from this hitch she had never once suspected in her friend's character. This hitch that explained so much. This inability to take responsibility for her own actions. For without that, she could never take the helm of her own destiny.

"Perhaps you might change your mind someday," she said at last. For two people who had once been eager to talk of subjects great and small, it was difficult to be reduced to small talk.

"Perhaps. Do give my regards to your most excellent Mr. Protheroe. I was quite taken with him."

Claire's maternal instincts leaped to attention. "Do not even think of pursuing Lewis. He is not in your league."

But Peony's insouciant smile, the public smile, was back. The breeze blew the feathers forward on her little tip-tilted hat, so that they veiled her eyes. "Don't worry. He is quite safe from me. Everything in trousers is, at the moment." Her mask of worldliness was firmly in place now. "But never fear. I shall recover."

"I hope so."

"Good-bye, Claire."

"Good-bye. I am sorry that we must part this way."

"Oh, you never know." Peony waved her gloved fingers. "The skies are full of surprises. And so am I."

Then she turned away, picked up her valise, and followed

the distant figures of Cyril and Charlotte toward the gate and the waiting cab.

Claire walked over to the landau, where Andrew was beginning the ignition sequence and the little boys were fidgeting and fighting in the rear compartment.

"Clary, hurry." Nicholas had poor Alfred by the ear. "It is time for us to go home."

"I quite agree." Andrew closed the lid of the boiler and held his arms open just wide enough for her to step into them.

"Will you pilot the landau today?" she said into his coat. "I am done in, and it is not even noon."

"But we are home, and safe, and together." His arms tightened around her. "I have learned during our travels that these are three gifts without price."

"Which you have made possible." She lifted her head and kissed him.

"Clary!"

Andrew laughed. "Come, let us be on our way before we have a mutiny on our hands. That plus piracy would be entirely too much for one morning."

He handed her in, settled next to her, let off the buildup of steam, and pushed out the acceleration bar.

As they passed through the gate, Cyril was just assisting Peony into the cab. Claire turned to look through the isinglass window, but though they passed quite close, she did not see anyone wave.

Andrew took her hand with his free one. "She will be all right."

"Are you certain?" Already she could feel the hollowness of loss in the pit of her belly.

"I am," her husband said. "And do you know why?"

"Because Peony always lands on her feet?"

"No." He squeezed her hand. "Because she is so much like you."

The landau picked up speed. And soon there was no longer any reason to look back, when those she loved were right here with her, and a glad welcome waited at home.

THE END

AFTERWORD

Dear reader,

Thank you so much for reading *Carrick House*. I hope you enjoyed this little trifle, and that you enjoy reading the adventures of Lady Claire and the gang in the Magnificent Devices world as much as I enjoy writing them. It is your support and enthusiasm that is like the steam in an airship's boiler, keeping the entire enterprise afloat and ready for the next adventure.

You might leave a review on your favorite retailer's site to tell others about the books. And you can find print, digital, and audiobook editions of the series online. I hope to see you over at my website, www.shelleyadina.com, where you can sign up for my newsletter and be the first to know of new releases and special promotions. You'll also receive a free short story set in the Magnificent Devices world just for subscribing!

To learn the dreadful circumstances of poor Emma Makepeace's passing, you might begin a new adventure with Daisy and Frederica Linden with the first book in the Mysterious Devices series, *The Bride Wore Constant White*, which is also set in the Magnificent Devices world.

Turn the page for an excerpt. Fair winds!

Shelley

EXCERPT

THE BRIDE WORE CONSTANT WHITE BY SHELLEY ADINA

July 1895
Bath, England

*I*t is a truth universally acknowledged that a young woman of average looks, some talent, and no fortune must be in want of a husband, the latter to be foisted upon her at the earliest opportunity lest she become an embarrassment to her family. This had been depressingly borne in upon Miss Margrethe Amelia Linden, known to her family and her limited number of intimate friends as Daisy, well before the occasion of her twenty-first birthday.

"Certainly you cannot go to a ball, escorted or not," said her Aunt Jane. "You are not out of mourning for your dear mother. It would not be suitable. I am surprised that you have even brought it up, Daisy."

Daisy took a breath in order to defend herself, but her aunt forestalled her with a raised salad fork.

"No, I will invite a very few to lunch—including one or

two suitable young men. Now that you have come into my sister's little bit of money, you will be slightly more attractive to a discerning person than, perhaps, you might have been before. Mr. Fetherstonehaugh, now. He still cherishes hopes of you, despite your appalling treatment of him. I insist on your considering him seriously. His father owns a manufactory of steambuses in Yorkshire, and he is the only boy in a family of five."

"I do not wish to be attractive to any of the gentlemen of our acquaintance, Aunt." *Particularly not to him.* "They lack gumption. To say nothing of chins."

This had earned her an expression meant to be crushing, but which only succeeded in making Aunt Jane look as though her lunch had not agreed with her.

"Your uncle and I wish to see you safely settled, dear," she said with admirable restraint.

Aunt Jane prided herself on her restraint under provocation. She had become rather more proud of it in the nearly two years since her sister had brought her two daughters to live under her roof, and then passed on to her heavenly reward herself. When one's sister's husband was known to have gone missing in foreign parts, one was also subject to impertinent remarks. Therefore, her restraint had reached heroic proportions.

"When you have been married fifty years, like our beloved Queen, you will know that a chin or lack thereof is hardly a consideration in a good husband—while a successful manufactory certainly is."

Daisy was not sure if Aunt Jane had meant to insult the prince, who from all accounts was still quite an attractive man. It was true that she could no more imagine Her Majesty without her beloved Albert than the sun without a moon. They had a scandalous number of children—nine!—and still the newspapers had reported that they had danced until dawn at Lord and Lady Dunsmuir's ball in London earlier in the week. Her Majesty was said to be prodigiously fond of dancing—between that and childbirth, she must be quite the athlete.

Daisy had never danced until dawn in her life, and doing so seemed as unlikely as having children.

Especially now.

For as of ten days ago, she was no longer a genteel spinster of Margaret's Buildings, Bath, but a woman of twenty-one years and independent means, having procured not only a letter of credit from her bank, but a ticket from Bath to London, and subsequently, passage aboard the packet to Paris, where she had boarded the transatlantic airship *Persephone* bound for New York.

"My goodness, you're so brave," breathed Emma Makepeace, her breakfast companion in the grand airship's dining saloon this morning, the third of their crossing. She had been listening with rapt attention, her spoonful of coddled egg halting in its fatal journey. "But at what point did you realize you were not alone?"

Daisy glanced at her younger sister, Frederica, who wisely did not lift her own attention from her plate, but continued to shovel in poached eggs, potatoes, and sliced ham glazed in orange sauce as though this were her last meal.

"As we were sailing over the Channel. At that point, my sister deemed it safe to reveal herself, since there would be no danger of my sending her back to our aunt and uncle." She gave a sigh. "We are committed to this adventure together, I am afraid."

"I certainly am," Freddie ventured. "I used all my savings for the tickets, including what I could beg from Maggie Polgarth."

"Who is that?" Miss Makepeace asked, resuming her own breakfast with a delicate appetite. "One of your school friends?"

Freddie nodded. "Maggie and her cousin Elizabeth Seacombe are the wards of Lady Claire Malvern, of Carrick House in Belgravia."

"Oh, I have met Lady Claire. Isn't she lovely? What an unexpected pleasure it is to meet people acquainted with her."

While Daisy recovered from her own surprise at a reliable third party knowing people she had half believed to be imaginary, Freddie went on.

"With Lady Claire's encouragement, both Maggie and Lizzie own shares in the railroads *and* the Zeppelin Airship Works, though they are only eighteen—my own age. But that is beside the point." Another glance at Daisy, who had been caught by the deep golden color of the marmalade in her spoon.

If she were to paint a still life at this very moment, she would use lemon yellow, with a bit of burnt umber, and some scarlet lake—just a little—for the bits of orange peel embedded deep within.

"The point?" Miss Makepeace inquired, and Daisy came back to herself under their joint regard. It was up to her to redirect the course of the conversation.

"The point is that, having had some number of astonishing adventures—I have my doubts about the veracity of some of them—Miss Polgarth was all too forthcoming in her encouragement of my sister's desertion of her responsibilities to school and family."

"You deserted yours, too," Freddie pointed out. "Poor Mr. Fetherstonehaugh. He is not likely to recover his heart very soon."

"Oh dear." Miss Makepeace was one of those fortunate individuals who would never have to settle for the chinless and suitable of this world. For she was a young woman of considerable looks and some means, despite the absence of anyone resembling a chaperone or a lady's maid. Perhaps that individual kept herself to her cabin. Her clothes were not showy, but so beautiful they made Daisy ache inside—the pleats perfection, the colors becoming, the lace handmade. Clearly her time in Paris before boarding *Persephone* had been well spent in purchasing these delights.

Miss Makepeace had been blessed with hair the shade of melted caramel and what people called an "English skin." Daisy, being as English as anyone, had one too by default, but hers didn't have the perfect shades of a rose petal. Nor did her own blue eyes possess that deep tint verging on violet. At least Daisy's hair could be depended on—reddish-brown in some lights and with enough wave in it to make it easy to put up— unlike poor Freddie, who had inherited Mama's lawless dark curls. No one would be clamoring at the door to paint Daisy, but Miss Makepeace—oh, she was a horse of a different color.

She absolutely must persuade her to sit for a portrait in watercolors.

But talk of poor Mr. Fetherstonehaugh had brought the ghost of a smile to their companion's face, so Daisy thought it prudent not to abandon the subject of gentlemen just yet, despite its uncomfortable nature. They had been in the air for three days, and after the second day, had found one another convivial enough company that they had begun looking for each other at meals, and spending the afternoons together embroidering or (in Daisy's case) sketching. The lavish interiors of *Persephone* fairly begged to be painted in her travel journal. In all that time Daisy had not seen Miss Makepeace smile. Not a real one. But now, one had nearly trembled into life, and she would use Mr. Fetherstonehaugh ruthlessly if it meant coaxing it into full bloom.

"Have you ever been to Bath, Miss Makepeace?" she asked, spreading marmalade on the toast.

"Only once, when I was a girl," she said. "Papa's business keeps him in London and New York nearly exclusively, and after Mama passed away, I did not have a companion with whom to go to such places. I remember it being very beautiful," she said wistfully. "And at the bottom of the Royal Crescent is a gravel walk. I wondered if it could be the very one where Captain Wentworth and Anne Elliot walked after all was made plain between them."

Frederica, being of a literal turn of mind, blinked at her. "They were not real, Miss Makepeace."

The English skin colored a little. "I know. But it was a pretty fancy, for the time it took me to walk down the hill to the gate."

"Poor Mr. Fetherstonehaugh," Daisy said on a sigh. "He attempted to quote Jane Austen to me while we were dancing in the parlor of one of my aunt's acquaintance three weeks ago."

"That sounds most promising in a man," Miss Makepeace said.

"But it was the first sentences of *Pride and Prejudice*, Miss Makepeace." She leaned in. "And they were said in reference *to himself.*"

To her delight, the smile she had been angling for blossomed into life. "Dear me. Miss Austen would be appalled."

"My sentiments exactly. And when he turned up on my aunt's doorstep the next morning proposing himself as the companion of my future life, I took my example from Elizabeth Bennet on the occasion of *her* first proposal. I fear the allusion was lost on him, however." She frowned. "He called me a heartless flirt."

Miss Makepeace covered her mouth with her napkin and Daisy could swear it was to muffle a giggle. "You are no such thing," she said when she could speak again. "I should say it was a near escape."

"Our aunt would not agree," Freddie put in. "She and my uncle have very strong feelings about indigent relations and their burden upon the pocketbook."

"Granted, it is not their fault their pocketbook is slender," Daisy conceded. "But that is no reason to push us on every gentleman who stops to smell the roses nodding over the wall."

"How do you come to be aboard *Persephone?*" Freddie asked their companion shyly.

She was not yet out, so had not had many opportunities to go about in company. Add to this a nearly paralyzing shyness —for reasons both sisters kept secret, and despite the misleading behavior of her hair—and it still astonished Daisy that she had had the gumption to follow her all the way to London with nothing but her second-best hat and a valise containing three changes of clothes, her diary, and a canvas driving coat against bad weather.

Now it was Miss Makepeace who leaned in, the lace covering her fine bosom barely missing the marmalade on her own toast. "Can you keep a secret?"

"Oh, yes," Freddie said eagerly.

Which was quite true. Among other things, she had concealed from everyone—except perhaps that deplorable Maggie Polgarth—her plans to run away and accompany Daisy on her mission.

"I am what is known as a mail-order bride." Miss Makepeace sat back to enjoy the effect of this confidence on her companions.

"A what?" Freddie said after a moment, when no clarification seemed to be forthcoming.

"There is no such thing," Daisy said a little flatly. Well, it was better than sitting and gaping like a flounder.

"There I must contradict you." Miss Makepeace aligned her knife and fork in the middle of her plate, and the waiter, seeing this signal, whisked it away. "In the guise of a literary club, I have been meeting these last six months in London with a group of young ladies determined to make their own fortunes. An agency assisted us in finding the best matches of ability and temperament in places as far-flung as the Canadas and the Louisiana Territory."

"There are agencies for this sort of thing?" Daisy managed under the shock of this fresh information. It was lucky that Aunt Jane was as ignorant of these facts as Daisy herself had been until this moment, or heaven knew where Daisy might have been shipped off to by now.

And what was a young woman like Miss Makepeace, with

every blessing of breeding and beauty, doing applying as a mail-order bride? It defied understanding.

Miss Makepeace nodded. "I have been writing to Mr. Bjorn Hansen, of Georgetown, for some months, and am convinced that he will make me a good husband." She touched the exceedingly modest diamond upon the fourth finger of her left hand. "He sent this in his last letter, and I sent my acceptance by return airship."

"My goodness," Freddie breathed. "I have never met a mail-order bride. I thought they only existed in the flickers—you know, like *Posted to Paradise*." She and Daisy had stood in the queue outside the nickelodeon on Milsom Street for half an hour to see that one, much to their aunt's disgust. But it had been so romantic!

"We are quite real, I assure you." Two dimples dented Miss Makepeace's cheeks. "My suit and veil are in my trunk. I will meet Mr. Hansen in person for the first time when I alight in Georgetown, and we will be married two days later in the First Presbyterian Church on Taos Street. It is all arranged."

"Where is Georgetown, exactly?" Daisy asked.

Not that it mattered—she and Frederica were bound for Santa Fe, on a quest that could not be postponed. Their father, Dr. Rudolph Linden, had been missing for nearly two years. Influenza had taken their mother last winter—hastened, Daisy was certain, by the anxiety and depression she had suffered after his mysterious disappearance. Now that she had reached her majority, Daisy was determined to take up the search where her mother had left off. And this time, if love and determination meant anything, she and Freddie would find him.

"It is in the northern reaches of the Texican Territories, in the mountains," Miss Makepeace explained in answer to her question. "From Denver, it is merely an hour west by train. It is said to be one of the loveliest towns in the territory—and certainly one of the richest. Silver, you know. It is surrounded by mines on every side, and has a bustling economy, I am told."

A young man who had been passing on the way to his table now hesitated next to theirs. "I do beg your pardon. Forgive me for intruding, but are you speaking of Georgetown?"

If Aunt Jane had been sitting opposite, Daisy had no doubt there would have been either the cut direct—or an invitation to breakfast if she thought the young man might be good husband material. But they were en route for a continent where one might stop and strike up a conversation without having to be formally introduced by a mutual acquaintance—or to give one's family antecedents back four generations.

"We are, sir. Do you know it?"

His square, honest face broke into a smile, and Daisy noted with interest the quality of the velvet lapels on his coat, and the fashionable leaf-brown color of his trousers—not the dull brown of earth, but the warmer tones of the forest in autumn.

"I am bound there as well. Please allow me to introduce myself. My name is Hugh Meriwether-Astor, originally from Philadelphia. I have recently bought a share in the Pelican mine."

"And are you going out to inspect your investment, or have you been there before?" Miss Makepeace asked.

"This is my first visit. I'm afraid I have an ulterior motive —that of escaping the bad temper of my older brother, who is not quite so conservative in his business dealings. I should like to get my hands dirty, and do a little excavating myself if I can, before I go back to law school. And you?"

As the eldest, and practically a married woman, Miss Makepeace made the introductions. Daisy noted that she did not vouchsafe any personal details of their voyage, she supposed because she had no personal observations of her future home to offer him. They parted with promises of seeing one another at the card tables after dinner, and the young man continued to his table by the viewing port.

"What a nice person," Frederica ventured. "He does not seem much older than you, Daisy, and yet he owns part of a mine. His family must be rather well off."

"If my facts are in order, he is closely connected to the Meriwether-Astor Manufacturing Works in Philadelphia," Miss Makepeace said in a low tone. Heaven forbid the young man should know they were discussing him. "Surely even in Bath you will have read in the papers about his cousin, Gloria Meriwether-Astor, who owns the company."

"It's a difficult name to miss," Daisy said. "Wasn't she the one who singlehandedly stopped a war in the Wild West and returned home in triumph with none other than a railroad baron's long-lost heir for a husband?"

Honestly, while it might have been quite true, it did sound like one of the sensational plots beloved of the flickers.

"I am sure it wasn't singlehandedly," Miss Makepeace said. "But I will say that the union of two such industrial fortunes made headlines in the Fifteen Colonies, and London and Zurich as well. It was all any of my father's cronies talked of at dinner for weeks."

"My friend Maggie knows her," Freddie said most unexpectedly. "Gloria, I mean. Mrs. Stanford Fremont."

"Nonsense," Daisy said. Honestly, she was becoming very tired of these references. "Another of that girl's absurd fabrications."

"It isn't!" Freddie drew back, affronted, and refused to speak for the rest of their meal.

There were some misfortunes for which one could only be thankful.

I HOPE you'll continue the adventure by purchasing *The Bride Wore Constant White.*

Thank you!

Shelley

ALSO BY SHELLEY ADINA

STEAMPUNK

The Magnificent Devices series

The Mysterious Devices series

The Bride Wore Constant White

The Dancer Wore Opera Rose

The Lady Wore Venetian Red

The Governess Wore Payne's Gray

The Judge Wore Lamp Black

The Soldier Wore Prussian Blue

ROMANCE

Moonshell Bay

Call For Me

Dream of Me

Reach For Me

Caught You Looking

Caught You Listening

Caught You Hiding

Corsair's Cove

Kiss on the Beach (Corsair's Cove Chocolate Shop 3)

Secret Spring (Corsair's Cove Orchard 4)

PARANORMAL

Immortal Faith

ABOUT THE AUTHOR

Shelley Adina is the author of 24 novels published by Harlequin, Warner, and Hachette, and more than a dozen more published by Moonshell Books, Inc., her own independent press. She writes steampunk and contemporary romance as Shelley Adina, and as Adina Senft, writes Amish women's fiction. She holds an MFA in Writing Popular Fiction from Seton Hill University, and is currently at work on a PhD in Creative Writing with Lancaster University in the UK. She won RWA's RITA Award® in 2005, and was a finalist in 2006. When she's not writing, Shelley is usually quilting, sewing historical costumes, or hanging out in the garden with her flock of rescued chickens.

Shelley loves to talk with readers about books, chickens, and costuming!
www.shelleyadina.com
shelley@shelleyadina.com